Linda felt Jamie's ... swiftly banished all ... wouldn't have been surprised if the man read minds as a sideline! Patients sometimes thought psychiatrists could see into their minds, but that wasn't so. What they could do was interpret a person's thoughts and feelings from body language or from conversation—as much from what the person didn't say as what she did, and Linda wondered how much of herself she had unwittingly given away. It wouldn't do to underestimate Jamie Grainger.

Suddenly feeling emotionally naked, she finished her sorbet, then refused his offer of coffee. 'I couldn't manage a coffee, really, but thank you for a wonderful meal—and good conversation,' she added sincerely. 'I've enjoyed myself.'

'More than you expected,' Jamie finished for her, and Linda coloured. There he was again, correctly interpreting her thoughts!

'Perhaps,' she admitted. 'Though I seem to have spent the evening talking about myself. I haven't heard any of your guilty secrets!' She spoke lightly, but his face clouded.

'I'm sorry—did I speak out of turn?' Her smile was contrite, and Jamie shrugged, then grinned lazily.

'I locked all my guilty secrets up years ago and threw away the key!' he said carelessly.

Hazel Fisher is a trained psychiatric nurse, but has also worked on medical and surgical wards in general hospitals. She draws on her own nursing experiences to provide the background for her novels, supplemented where necessary by careful research. She is half-Geordie but has spent most of her life in Sussex, and now lives in a pretty little village nestling at the foot of the South Downs. She enjoys reading and writing Medical Romances.

Previous Title

CALL AN ANGEL

A DREAM WORTH SHARING

BY

HAZEL FISHER

MILLS & BOON LIMITED

ETON HOUSE   18–24 PARADISE ROAD
RICHMOND   SURREY   TW9 1SR

First published in Great Britain 1990
by Mills & Boon Limited

© Hazel Fisher 1990

Australian copyright 1990
Philippine copyright 1991
This edition 1991

ISBN 0 263 77143 1

Set in 10 on 11½ pt Linotron Plantin
03-9102-57209
Typeset in Great Britain by Centracet, Cambridge
Made and printed in Great Britain

CHAPTER ONE

'AND how do you feel now you've survived your first week, Sister?' Nurse Craig asked. 'Always the worst, that first week, no matter where you are,' the buxom staff nurse went on, and Linda Scott smiled a trifle ruefully.

'I know—everything that *can* happen usually does! One way and another, it's been quite a week,' Linda admitted, gathering up the reports on the day patients. 'It's a challenge, though, and I never could resist that! Now, is there anything I've forgotten?'

Nurse Craig shook her head. 'No, you've given me all the notes, I think. Oh— what about Mrs Skilton? She's been referred again.'

'The lady with agoraphobia? No, she didn't show up. What happens when a patient doesn't attend? Are we responsible for finding out why, or does the social worker visit?'

'Usually the social worker or the community nurse, though sometimes our Jamie turns up on their doorstep unexpectedly and charms them into coming! Pity you've missed him this week. Still, you must have seen him at the interview?' the nurse went on, clearly dying for any little titbit of information about the handsome, charming and utterly chauvinistic Dr Jamie Grainger!

As far as Linda could see, the sun shone out of his eyes, the moon rose at his bidding, and blossoms grew in profusion where'er he walked! At least, that was the impression she got whenever anyone at the Summerheath

5

Clinic mentioned the consultant psychiatrist by name. Her view of him was rather different, but it would be unprofessional of her to say so.

'Yes, Dr Grainger interviewed me. He's very enthusiastic about the Clinic,' she said, striving to be fair. After all, she had no quarrel with his professional abilities—it was only his personality she found objectionable. And how!

The nurse beamed. 'He's enthusiastic about everything to do with the day patients. Says this is the psychiatry of the future, for the sort of people we treat, anyway. Better than hauling them off to a Victorian workhouse miles from home and family. He's had some wonderful results,' she added, 'and the patients absolutely adore him!'

'Yes, I've noticed,' Linda said carefully, then rose, pushing back a tendril of long, silvery blonde hair as she did so. The weather was hot and humid, and it would have been cooler for her if she could have worn her hair in its usual neat style instead of loose, but orders were orders. Dr Grainger liked a certain amount of informality at the clinic and insisted that nursing staff didn't wear uniform. Only the professional standards of psychiatric nursing remained unyieldingly high and formal.

'I'll just leave a note for Doctor about Mrs Skilton,' Nurse Craig was saying. 'Since she's not likely to venture out of doors without support, he might go himself. He likes to——'

'What do I like to?' a deep voice broke in, and Linda felt waves of colour suffuse her cheeks, though why, she couldn't imagine. It wasn't as if they had been discussing the psychiatrist behind his back. It was absurd to feel guilty, but she did, and she resented it.

His cool glance swept over her now, and there was a

gleam in those light grey eyes that boded ill for someone, but he was all smiles when he greeted Muriel Craig, who was obviously a favourite with him.

'Sister and I were just talking about you—weren't we, Sister?' Nurse Craig added, making matters worse. 'She was saying how enthusiastic you were about the Clinic!'

'Why, thank you, Sister Scott,' said Dr Grainger, essaying a little bow, and Linda forced a smile, mistrusting his affable manner. Of course, psychiatrists were people who kept their own emotions well in hand, and there was unlikely to be any open hostility between them no matter how great their differences of opinion, but that charming smile hid a will of iron—no, a will of steel, and there was trouble ahead. Linda could feel it in her very bones.

They stood surveying each other, and for a moment, it was as if Nurse Craig ceased to exist. Linda shivered slightly, then tore her gaze away, pretending to be searching for something amongst the notes on her desk. 'Mrs Gwen Skilton didn't attend this morning, Doctor. Will you be paying a domiciliary visit or should I refer her to the social worker?' she said in the waiting silence.

'I think a home visit's an excellent idea of yours, Sister. Why don't we both go?' he suggested gently, and Linda was at a loss for words for a moment. 'About now might be a good idea—unless you're anxious to get away home?' he added, a little smile hovering about his firm mouth.

'No, no, there's no hurry—I'm a free agent,' Linda hurried on, then felt a stab of resentment at the way the doctor's brows rose a fraction. Well, of course they would, wouldn't they? Just because he'd seen her bidding Paul Winterton a fond farewell, he supposed all sorts of untrue things about her private life. Her chin lifted a little, and those light eyes laughed at her, but he didn't comment, merely held open the office door, and an indignant Linda hurried to the staff-room to collect her personal belongings. The last thing she wanted was to spend the next hour or so in the company of Dr Jamie Grainger, but it seemed she had no choice.

She stole a quick glance at herself in the mirror, noting with annoyance her flushed cheeks and over-bright eyes. Hastily she ran a comb through her fine, wayward hair, renewed her lipstick, then made a final check in the mirror. The petite girl in the summer dress who gazed back at her was hardly the picture of a mature, experienced psychiatric nurse, but at twenty-five Linda had no doubts about her ability to cope with the taxing job of day patient sister. Her clear blue eyes grew shadowed for a moment. No, work wasn't the problem. Apart from wondering what to do about Paul, the only cloud on her horizon at the moment was her new chief—she had the feeling the cloud would darken and turn into a full-blown storm!

Silently reproving her reflection, Linda picked up her bag and hurried out into the sunshine.

There was no cooling breeze today, and she still felt hot and flustered as she and the psychiatrist walked side by side towards the small car park. It was an effort to keep up with him, since he made no allowance for her much shorter legs, but she was determined to, no matter what. As they reached his Jaguar, he turned to her, still with that little smile on his lips. 'You're out of breath, Sister. I would have slowed down if you'd asked!'

Linda tried not to smile back, but she could see the humour of the situation as she admitted, 'I was determined not to ask! I hate allowances being made for me just because I'm short,' she added sweetly, and he chuckled.

For a moment he actually seemed human, though she knew he wasn't. Hadn't he lectured her on the need for senior nurses—and doctors—to have private lives that were beyond reproach? All without knowing the facts of her relationship with Paul. The man wasn't human at all! He was a killjoy, a prude. He was utterly——

'Are you proposing to run alongside the car, Sister, or will you join me inside?'

Feeling foolish, Linda marshalled her thoughts. A domiciliary visit to a patient wasn't the place to tell the hateful Dr Grainger *exactly* what she thought of his interference in her life, but the time would come.

The Summerheath Clinic was set in its own beautifully kept grounds only a few minutes from the sea at Little Upwell in Sussex, and as they emerged from the short, gravelled drive, Linda could see the English Channel straight ahead, the sun sparkling on the water, seabirds dipping and weaving overhead. As Dr Grainger turned the car into Channel Road, the sea was on their right all the way along, and at last she found some respite from the heat. It was on days like this that she was glad she no longer had to wear a thick, uncomfortable uniform, but somehow she never really felt like a nurse in her own clothes. This was a minor point of contention with the doctor, but today she was glad of his insistence on informality.

'How did your first week go, Sister—or may I call you Linda?' Dr Grainger broke into her thoughts.

Surprised, she said, 'Yes, of course you can call me Linda, and the week went very well, I think. Though things at the Summerheath are rather different from my last hospital,' she went on carefully.

'Such as?' he asked, then swore as a jaywalker decided to stroll across towards the sea, and Linda smothered a laugh. Perhaps he *was* human, after all!

'At the Baxter, patients were called "clients", so I started off on the wrong foot by calling one lady that. She told me that only probation officers and social workers had clients. She was a patient and I was a nurse and that was that.' Linda paused, her silence inviting comment, but Dr Grainger stared straight ahead, seemingly concentrating on the road, which was busy as the small resort woke up for the benefit of its summer visitors.

As the silence continued, Linda decided to carry on with the list of minor setbacks she had encountered. 'I lost two patients on Wednesday—that was at the clinic for obsessive-compulsive problems. Of course they turned up, but I got in a bit of a panic remembering that Beachy Head is so near.'

'You'll find it's usually strangers who choose Beachy Head as their last resting place,' the doctor commented as he slowed the big car, then stopped outside a neat row of terraced houses. 'Here we are. Let's pop in and see if we can help Mrs Skilton come to terms with her disability. For that's what it is,' he added.

On a day like this, to remain shut away indoors because you couldn't face either people or open spaces was certainly a disability, but one that was more common than lay people might think. Linda glanced speculatively at the tall doctor beside her as they waited at the front door, wondering how he would handle the situation, and whether he was as good at his job as the elderly consultant with whom she had worked in London.

After a lengthy pause, the door was inched open by a tall, stooped man who peered at them. 'Oh, it's you,

Doctor! Come in—the wife's not bin well again. Always somethink, it is,' he added as he showed them into a rather dark sitting-room. 'Like some tea, would you?'

Without consulting her, Dr Grainger accepted for them both. 'There's nothing like a cuppa,' he commented, then eased his powerful body into a chair and closed his eyes, seemingly at peace with the world. Clearly he wasn't about to seek out their patient, and for a moment Linda wondered whether she was expected to do it for him. If she had been on her own, she would have done so once the tea had been brought, but since she was accompanying a consultant, it was up to him to make the first move. Any precipitate action on her part could ruin things.

'Is Mrs Skilton not joining us for tea?' the doctor asked as Mr Skilton carefully wheeled in a trolley. When Linda rose, prepared to ask if she might pour, Dr Grainger waved her down, his eyes never leaving the old man's face.

Mr Skilton looked away, then shrugged and indicated the teapot. 'Don't let the tea get cold, Doctor. I'll see if I can winkle the missus out,' he added, shuffling towards the door.

'Tell her I'm taking Sister Scott out to dinner, so we haven't much time,' Dr Grainger called after him, and Mr Skilton turned, clearly surprised.

'Right you are then, Doctor. Shan't be a jiffy.'

That was too much, and Linda's gaze was reproachful. 'That's rather unkind, Doctor. When Mrs Skilton finds out it's not true, she'll——'

'Not true? Of course it's true,' he said smoothly. 'You told me you were a free agent, that you didn't need to hurry home. So why can't I take you out to dinner?' he went on conversationally.

Before Linda could think of a suitably crushing reply, Mr Skilton returned, his wife hovering behind him, and she put all thoughts of personal animosities out of her mind. The patient and her needs were all that mattered. The fact that Jamie Grainger was a bossy, self-opinion-ated swine was totally irrelevant!

Try as she might, she couldn't fault his technique. He was patience itself with the nervous little woman, and not once did he reproach her for not attending the day clinic. The community psychiatric nurse was supposed to take her to the clinic, but Mrs Skilton confessed that she'd hidden until the nurse had gone.

'Wasn't I awful, Doctor?' she whispered, holding on to the psychiatrist's hand as if to a lifeline, and he turned the full force of his charm upon her. Linda smiled to herself as she saw Mrs Skilton's resistance melting by the minute. Nurse Craig was right—Jamie Grainger *could* charm patients into doing things they didn't want to do! Charming a nurse into dining with him was another matter, though, and Linda was determined that he wouldn't be so successful!

After extracting a promise from the patient that she would attend the following week if someone called for her, Dr Grainger smiled disarmingly at Linda herself, who eyed him warily, wondering what was coming next.

'Sister Scott here will call to see you on Monday— won't you, Sister?' His eyes challenged Linda, who found herself agreeing.

'Of course I will. What time will you be ready, my love?' she asked Mrs Skilton, holding out her hand.

Gwen Skilton hung on to it, the way she had grasped the doctor's only moments before. Body contact was important in psychiatry, and too often patients had no one to whom they could hold on, no one to offer reassurance or a listening ear. That was what it was all about as far as those with nervous disorders went, and Linda felt they had both got through to Mrs Skilton, letting her know they wanted her company, needed her at the Clinic.

'A successful visit, I think,' Dr Grainger commented as he opened the car door for her. Mrs Skilton hadn't been able to see them to the door, but she was watching from a window, and Linda turned to wave to her.

'Yes, I think so,' she agreed. 'She's a nice little soul. She's had treatment before, I suppose?'

'Mm, quite a lot, but still the fear comes back. The behaviour therapy worked up to a point. We got her actually going out with a therapist. Then she regressed, but we're not quite back to square one, so there's hope. The family situation is awkward, though. Her married daughter despises her and her husband thinks she's shamming half the time. You've had more experience with compulsions, haven't you?'

'Yes, we did quite a lot of that at the Baxter. It's alarming how many otherwise normal people have to go back umpteen times to check that they've turned off the gas or closed the windows, or have to perform elaborate rituals before dressing or going to bed. And they've often no one to talk to about it,' Linda went on reflectively.

'That's where *we* come in. I find that type of patient—or client, if you like—a refreshing change from the psychotic illnesses like schizophrenia or manic-depression. These are people who can be cured, or at least enabled to lead a fairly normal life once the crippling symptoms have gone. That's the plus side of psychiatry. It makes up for the people we can't help, the people no one can cure,' Dr Grainger said, a note of sadness in his voice that made Linda wonder if there was someone like that among his own family or friends—someone he had tried to help but failed.

'I'll drop you at your cottage,' he was saying, and Linda hurriedly brought her thoughts back to the problem in hand—how to tell the consultant psychiatrist that she didn't, but definitely did *not*, want to dine with him!

'Thank you, Doctor, but I——' she began, but wasn't allowed to finish.

'Call me Jamie, since we're off duty. Or will that be more than you can cope with?' he went on, a chuckle in his voice.

'I think I can manage that,' she agreed tightly, not letting him see how he'd ruffled her feathers. He seemed determined to do that at every turn, though she might have been misjudging the man. It was probably just a clash of personalities and would eventually sort itself out.

'Here we are, safe and sound.'

Linda looked about her in surprise. 'Oh, we're here already? But I'm nearly ten miles out of town—there's a short cut I didn't know about!' she exclaimed.

'I know all the short cuts hereabouts. I used to spend holidays here as a boy—had an aunt in Brighton,' Jamie explained.

'Well, thank you again, Doc—Jamie,' she amended swiftly, wondering how she was to get back to the Clinic on Monday morning. Surely he didn't expect her to walk ten miles? He looked a fresh-air fiend, and one of the nurses had told her he had his own gym and swimming pool.

Before he could get out and open the door for her, Linda had extricated herself from the car, then stood eyeing him uncertainly. Being a direct sort of person, she felt she must tell him she didn't want his company, and not wrap it up in too much flannel, but she found something appealing in the wistful little smile on his face, the little-boy-lost expression in his eyes. It was deliberate, of course. The man must know the effect he had on women, but even so she couldn't bring herself to hurt him. So, swallowing her pride, she meekly asked what time she was to be ready.

The smile broadened. 'Did you decide you couldn't bear to hurt my tender feelings?' he asked softly, those mesmerising eyes half closed.

In a romantic novel, it would have been called a sensuous look, and that was exactly what it was. The man was too attractive for his own good—and for her peace of mind! 'I thought it only prudent to accept my chief's invitation, yes,' she said coolly. 'Will seven o'clock be all right? I need time to run a bath and——'

'Let's say a quarter past, then. Enjoy your bath, Sister Scott!' With a wave, he got back into the car, reversed away neatly along the little lane that led to the six terraced cottages, then was gone from Linda's sight.

She remained where she was for a long moment, wondering how she was to work with the man. He was the type of man who took people over, moulded them to *his* way of thinking, *his* way of doing things, something she found totally unacceptable. Well, just let him try to mould her and he would find that he had met his match!

Wearing that determined expression her friends would have recognised, Linda marched indoors, and reflected wryly that she was already doing the psychiatrist's bidding—dining with him when, a few minutes before, she'd had no such intention!

They dined in Brighton, at a little restaurant attached to one of the seafront hotels—a restaurant where Dr Grainger appeared to be very well known. Linda sup-

pressed a smile as they were almost reverently escorted
down the steps to the cellar-like restaurant, then gasped
at the scene before her. It was decked out as Neptune's
Cave, the stone walls festooned with artificial seaweed,
with wide swathes of fishermen's netting draped here
and there, and nautical murals painted on one wall, the
tables themselves being plain and unvarnished and only
dimly lit by the alcove lights.

It wasn't too crowded, and they were shown to a table
right at the back of the cellar, Jamie suggesting Linda sit
facing the room to get a good view of the proceedings.
'There's a small cabaret occasionally,' he told her, evidently enjoying her surprise at her surroundings.
'Nothing much, a local group, a few songs with a guitar,
that sort of thing. Unfortunately the tourists have found
it, and it can get pretty crowded sometimes.' He smiled
lazily across at her, and Linda found herself returning
the smile. He was putting himself out to be pleasant, so
the least she could do would be to respond—surely she
could manage that for a couple of hours?

'Naturally the seafood's out of this world,' he went
on, 'but they do vegetarian dishes if you've a mind. And
how about melon to start?'

'Melon would be lovely, thank you,' Linda agreed,
gazing about her.

They settled on salmon for the main course, the
youthful waiter drifted away, and they were alone. Of
course, there was the hubbub of the restaurant, the
occasional guffaw of laughter, the chink of cutlery and
glasses, yet Linda had the feeling they were alone. It was
eerie, and quickly she brushed the feeling aside, before
smiling over at Jamie. 'Thank you for bringing me here.
It's certainly different!'

'It's a bit artificial, I suppose, but it's a friendly place and I thought you would like it. Now,' he commanded, 'tell me about yourself.'

Linda put down her wine glass and glanced up sharply. Across the table, their eyes met, but there was nothing in his expression to which she could take exception. 'There's nothing much to tell, really,' she said carefully. 'I trained at Guy's, then went on to do my mental training at the Baxter. And there I stayed! It was good experience.'

'You've found it useful to have a general certificate as well as a psychiatric one?' he asked, and seemed genuinely interested in her reply. Under his gentle probing, Linda found herself giving him her opinion on the differences between the two trainings, and on the way psychiatry might develop in the future, and was amazed to find they were still conversing amiably by the time the pudding was brought—raspberry sorbet for her and a plain vanilla ice for Jamie.

If she was honest, she would have to admit she had enjoyed herself immensely. Unlike Paul, with this man there was no skirting around subjects that might upset him, no careful choice of words before they were uttered, and she found it refreshing. Then she felt Jamie's speculative gaze on her again, and swiftly banished all thoughts of Paul Winterton—she wouldn't have been surprised if the man read minds as a sideline! Patients sometimes thought psychiatrists could see into their minds, but that wasn't so. What they could do was interpret a person's thoughts and feelings from body language or from conversation—as much from what the person didn't say as what she did, and Linda wondered how much of herself she had unwittingly given away. It wouldn't do to underestimate Jamie Grainger.

Suddenly feeling emotionally naked, she finished her

sorbet, then refused his offer of coffee. 'I couldn't manage a coffee, really, but thank you for a wonderful meal—and good conversation,' she added sincerely. 'I've enjoyed myself.'

'More than you expected,' Jamie finished for her, and Linda coloured. There he was again, correctly interpreting her thoughts!

'Perhaps,' she admitted. 'Though I seem to have spent the evening talking about myself. I haven't heard any of *your* guilty secrets!' She spoke lightly, but his face clouded.

'I'm sorry—did I speak out of turn?' Her smile was contrite, and Jamie shrugged, then grinned lazily.

'I locked all my guilty secrets up years ago and threw away the key!' he said carelessly, then glanced at his watch. 'It doesn't look as though there's any cabaret this evening, so it's time we called it a day. You'll want to hurry home, I expect?'

Linda ignored the question in his voice. 'Yes, I think I ought to. I'm going away for the weekend and I'll have to make an early start tomorrow.' Quite why she told him that, she wasn't sure, but the air of friendliness vanished, to be replaced by a cool, professional smile.

'Then we'd better hurry,' was his only comment, as he waved an arm energetically for the bill, this seeming to be the accepted mode of attracting the waiters' attention.

As the waiter approached, Linda noticed a couple in the opposite corner who were trying to catch Jamie's eye. Then the woman came over, tall and reed-slim, in a clinging emerald gown that was a perfect foil for her red hair.

'Jamie—it *is* you! Robert said it couldn't be because that wasn't dear Wanda with you, but I said I was sure it was, and I've been proved right!' she finished smugly, her searching glance on Linda.

Jamie seemed happy enough to introduce them, and to Linda's surprise he didn't tell the woman she was a member of his staff. 'Jenny, this is Linda Scott—Linda, Jenny Meacham. The Meachams are old friends of mine,' he added.

Cold hazel eyes assessed Linda and evidently found her wanting, for Mrs Meacham's smile was brief. 'And where do you fit in, Miss Scott?' she asked. 'Jamie dear, you must bring Miss Scott to a little party we're giving at the end of the month. It's Robert's birthday, but that's only an excuse—I felt like giving a party anyway!'

'Thank you, Jenny. If work permits, I'm sure Linda and I will be happy to attend.' Jamie's expression gave nothing away, but Linda almost squirmed in her embarrassment. And who, she wondered, was Wanda?

Evidently Jenny Meacham remembered Wanda, for she clapped a hand to the side of her face in a theatrical gesture. 'Forgive me, Jamie! Of course, you'll be bringing Wanda—or isn't she well?'

'She was perfectly well the last time I saw her,' Jamie said amiably, and perhaps only Linda heard the steel beneath the polite words. 'Now, if you'll excuse me——'

'Of course, of course! Don't mind me, darlings, you hurry away!' She bent and kissed Jamie on the brow, then fluttered off.

'You must be wondering where Jenny's broomstick is,' he said lightly, then laughed at the dismayed expression on Linda's face.

'Well, I may have been!' she admitted, all the while wondering how he would extricate himself from the invitation to take her to that dreadful woman's party.

Whoever Wanda was, she obviously had prior claim to that doubtful privilege. The psychiatrist was divorced, Linda knew that much, but no one had mentioned a woman in his life at present. Perhaps if she had shown more appreciation of the news hot from the Clinic grapevine, someone would have mentioned the mysterious Wanda, but she'd made it clear she wasn't interested in the private lives of doctors or nurses, and only of patients where it obviously affected their disorders.

The journey back was completed virtually in silence, Jamie offering to drive her straight to the Clinic so that she could pick up her car. Linda occupied herself gazing through the window at the lights of Brighton as they passed through. It was like fairyland, and she watched wistfully as couples strolled in apparent harmony, with linked arms or hand in hand. Then they were on the open road. The dreams she had of being part of a normal love affair disintegrated as they left the lights behind. No, even if she loved him, life with Paul could never be like that; he was too vulnerable, too unsure of himself, too—well, yes, it had to be said: too dependent upon her and upon whoever else he could get to shoulder his burdens. It was a depressing feature, yet how could she let him down?

'Don't let Jenny get to you that much,' Jamie put in as they approached the small level crossing that marked the boundary of Little Upwell.

'Mm? Oh, no. I'd forgotten her. Really,' Linda assured him, rousing herself from her dark thoughts. 'I expect she's all right when you get to know her.'

'She is, actually.' He switched off the engine, prepared for a long wait at the crossing. 'She's got a kind heart under that brittle exterior.'

'Yes, I'm sure she has,' Linda agreed, and felt his silent laughter.

'I'll take Wanda to that party Jenny was on about,' he continued, as if she hadn't spoken. 'They understand each other, and Wanda will probably enjoy herself. You wouldn't—and quite frankly, neither shall I,' he admitted.

But you'll go because Wanda will enjoy it. Wanda and Jenny Meacham are two of a kind, so everyone will have a good time, except you, Linda mused, idly watching as the train made its slow way towards Hastings.

'It's about time civilisation came to this place,' Jamie commented as the gates swung slowly open. 'They're closed more often than they're open, I think.'

'So I gather. Everyone at the clinic made sure I knew about the crossing, and I learned several ways of avoiding it on my way from cottage to clinic!'

'They're nice little cottages. Inclined to be a bit damp in the winter, so keep a fire going,' he advised, then they were at the clinic, and Linda turned to him with a warm smile, but her words of thanks died on her lips at the expression in his eyes. It looked very much as if he wanted to kiss her, but he didn't, merely touched his hand against her cheek and wished her a pleasant goodnight.

'Goodnight, Jamie—and thank you again!' With an effort, Linda kept her voice steady.

'The pleasure was mine—all mine, probably,' he said wryly. 'Enjoy your weekend.'

When at last she got home, the cottage seemed empty and rather lonely without Jamie, but that was ridiculous, Linda told herself. He'd never been inside her home, so how could it be lonely without him?

Yet it was his grey eyes she saw in her dreams, and his

was the crisp dark hair she nestled against as their lips met in a kiss of such searing passion that Linda awoke suddenly, believing him to be lying there beside her. Startled, she sat up. The dream had been so vivid, Jamie's kisses so ardent, so loving. . . But she didn't even *like* the man!

Vigorously thumping the pillows to relieve her feelings, she settled back to try to sleep, but already the birds were twittering, and she lay there listening to them, tired but sleepless as Saturday dawned.

CHAPTER TWO

MONDAY was grey and chillier than of late, but Linda welcomed the change in the weather. A grey day suited her mood better, for Paul had telephoned her late on Sunday evening, and all her problems had come flooding back at the sound of his voice.

So engrossed in her thoughts was she that Jamie Grainger was almost past before she acknowledged his presence. Swiftly she pulled herself together. 'Good morning, Dr Grainger! I'm sorry—I was miles away,' she admitted.

At this time in the morning, the corridor of the Summerheath was crowded with staff hurrying to work, but Jamie ignored the people milling around them. His hand shot out and grasped her wrist and gave it a little shake. 'This is Monday morning, Sister Scott. Whatever happened during your weekend, forget it! You're paid to devote your time and thoughts to the patients on Mondays, so please try to remember that,' he went on brusquely, and Linda gasped at the unfairness of it all.

Honesty compelled her to admit that, from his point of view, it wasn't unfair. All he could see was a young woman daydreaming about the idyllic weekend she had just spent with her lover. Well, let him think that! It was none of his business where—or with whom—she spent her off duty. 'I'm very sorry, Doctor. You're quite right—now, may I have my wrist back?' Her voice was cold, but he seemed unaware of it and for a second or two his long, sensitive fingers caressed her wrist, his thumb probing her pulse-spot. Linda held her breath, fearful that he would sense the effect his nearness had on her. It wasn't fair! He had no right! Wrenching her hand free, she continued on her way, deaf to everyone and everything except the wild pounding of her heart, the racing of her pulse. Damn the man!

Once inside the sanctuary of her office, she flipped open the pages of her diary. Monday—collect Gwen Skilton and bring her in for an informal visit. Get permission to call for her again on Friday for the agoraphobic clinic. Well, she would try, but she doubted her ability to get the woman out of the house. It was clearly a case for the charming Dr Grainger!

Apart from that one visit, there were just the usual day patient activities to oversee—occupational therapy, the initial medical examination of new patients, relaxation classes. . . I could certainly do with a relaxation class, Linda thought grimly as she began to tackle the mountain of paperwork that was the lot of ward sisters at the Clinic. There was only the one nursing officer, and he seemed to have nothing more to do than carry important-looking papers around with him, dumping bits of them on everyone else's desk whenever he got the chance.

He must, Linda decided, have been around early this morning. Wearily she ran her fingers through her hair, then rummaged in a drawer, seeking a rubber band to keep the hair off her face. She was having a typical Monday morning feeling, but it had nothing to do with the job. Jamie Grainger's remark still rankled, and she wondered if he was as fault-finding with the other staff.

'Ah, here you are! Good morning to you, Sister.' Muriel Craig beamed at her, obviously not having a Monday morning feeling, and Linda smiled ruefully.

'Is it a good morning? Perhaps it will get better—ah!' She pounced on the elusive rubber band and ruthlessly pulled her hair through it, causing Nurse Craig to wince.

'Don't do that, Sister! Such lovely hair. What wouldn't I give to be a blonde!' The nurse tugged at her own shortish grey hair.

'I feel like having it chopped off, but——' Linda didn't finish the sentence. Paul liked her hair long, said it made her look like a mermaid. 'We'd better get on, I suppose,' she sighed, aware that the other nurse was giving her a sharp look. 'Have I the time to visit Mrs Skilton before lunch, I wonder? Oh, isn't Dr Ahmed doing the medicals this morning?'

'Yes, that's right. Only the two, though. You never know how long he's going to be, that's the only trouble. He usually takes a full history from them as well. You know the sort of thing?'

Linda nodded. 'Yes, when the symptoms started, what relation they bear to any upsets, family history, that sort of thing. I'd better leave Mrs Skilton until after lunch,' she decided, then went on to discuss the day patients' programme for the day.

Day patients usually attended from about nine until four, though some stayed later. Jamie had told her that if they wanted to stay, he certainly wasn't going to show them the door. As he said, sometimes it was a job to get them to attend in the first place!

It was lunchtime before she saw Jamie again, at least to speak to. He was usually about the Clinic, letting himself be seen, letting the patients know he was available at any time to listen to their problems, but his route this morning hadn't taken him anywhere near her, and for that she was grateful.

He wasn't to be avoided in the canteen, though, and

Linda tensed as his tall figure headed purposefully towards her table—a table she'd been sharing with Nurse Craig only moments before. Now she was alone and vulnerable, and her eyes were wary as he approached.

He paused to speak to one of the day patients, since patients as well as staff used the canteen, then he was beside her, and carefully Linda made room for him, watching in silence as he unloaded his tray. The salad he'd chosen looked totally insufficient for such a big man, and even the helping of new potatoes was minuscule. 'On a diet, Doctor?' she asked gently, as he sat down opposite her.

He followed her gaze. 'It doesn't look much, does it? Still, I usually eat well at night,' he added, with an urbane smile.

Taking it to mean that he was dining out with Wanda tonight, Linda merely smiled and concentrated on her pudding, a light fruit jelly. 'There's one thing, the food's very good here,' she commented as she finished the jelly, and his eyes narrowed.

'Only one thing, Sister?' he probed, and she flushed, wishing she had chosen her words more carefully.

'You know what I mean. You're being deliberately irritating today,' she added unwisely, then felt the chill in the atmosphere.

'If asking you to concentrate upon the patients rather than upon your trendy lover is being irritating, well, yes, I suppose I am,' was his only comment, and Linda bit back the words she wanted to hurl at him.

Instead she said quietly, 'Paul isn't my lover, Doctor.' Then a patient came to their table to speak to Jamie, and the moment of danger passed. He was right, she reflected later—keep your mind on the patients and you can't go wrong.

Mrs Skilton proved every bit as difficult to winkle out of her home as Linda had feared, and she had to spend most of the afternoon with the woman. In the end, fortified by her fifth cup of tea, Mrs Skilton managed to see Linda to the door and they stood together, gazing out across the street to where, if two more rows of houses hadn't been in the way, they would have seen the sea.

'Has it been long since you've seen the sea?' Linda asked casually as she prepared to leave.

Mrs Skilton shrugged. 'I can't say, Sister, and that's a fact. It's been a fair while. Still, it'll always be there, won't it?'

'Yes, that's true, but if you never come out, other people will be enjoying the sea view and you'll be as deprived as any slum dweller in the big cities, won't you? Yet you've got the sea practically on your doorstep,' Linda pointed out. 'Will you walk to the gate with me? I'll see that nothing happens to you.'

Still Mrs Skilton hesitated, and Linda could almost see her warring with herself, trying to pluck up the courage to take that one big step. And it was a big step to someone like that. Outside lurked unknown dangers while inside the house was a sanctuary, a haven, somewhere she couldn't be hurt or upset.

Eventually she managed to walk down the two steps at the front door, her hand clasping Linda's tightly. But there she stuck and couldn't be persuaded to move any further.

'All right, we'll leave it for now. Don't worry about it,' Linda said gently. 'You've done very well. Perhaps next time I come, you can walk a little way down the path with me?' she suggested.

'I'll try, Sister, that I will,' Mrs Skilton assured her, but Linda had her doubts.

It was obviously time for the psychologist to map out a new programme for her. At some hospitals there was a nurse-therapist who set out a selection of tasks for the phobic and obsessional patients to perform, though at the Summerheath this work was co-ordinated by the psychologist. The list was made with the co-operation of the patient herself, but the patient had to *want* to improve. Self-help and motivation were of vital importance, and Linda had the suspicion that Mrs Skilton didn't want to be rid of her phobia. If she could manipulate Jamie into admitting her, so much the better. It would prove to her husband and daughter that she really *did* have a serious disorder, and give her some of the sympathy and attention she obviously craved. But manipulating Jamie Grainger was a task far beyond anyone's ability, Linda was sure of that!

While she was in the vicinity, Linda thought she would call on a patient who was due to start at one of the obsessive-compulsive clinics. Most of the people who attended were out at work all day, though sometimes their symptoms were so debilitating that they could work only part-time, and of course sometimes they lost their jobs altogether. Often, though, they managed to run their lives normally, at least on the surface, holding down a job as well as getting through the domestic chores.

The new patient, Miss Anstey, was probably at work, and Linda put her card through the letterbox. She'd written a personal message on the card, letting Miss Anstey know she was welcome to contact her, or the Clinic at any time.

It was well after five by the time she returned to the Clinic, and the patients had all gone, at least the day patients had, but attached to the Clinic was a small in-patient unit, and Jamie was coming from that direction as Linda paused at the door of her office. He was grim-faced, and with a sinking heart she watched his approach. *Now* what had she done?

'Would you ask your—friend—to telephone you during your off-duty hours, Sister?' he began, and when Linda opened her mouth to protest, he hurried on, 'I can't imagine what you see in such an effeminate crea-ture, but he wants you to ring him urgently. The number's on your desk,' he added, already past her.

Linda closed her mouth again, hardly able to believe she'd heard right. Effeminate, indeed! Whatever was wrong with Paul, he certainly wasn't that! On the contrary, he had his full quota of healthy male appetite—something which was beginning to cause problems.

Shrugging the worry aside, Linda entered her office, threw her bag into a corner and sank down on to her comfortable swivel chair. What on earth could Paul want? And *why* did he have to ring when Jamie was about! Well, he could wait. No way was she going to phone him from the Clinic. The less the Clinic staff knew about her private life, the better.

Deciding to use the time to catch up on her paper-work, she bent her head over her notes, and was busily scribbling her comments when the psychiatrist reappeared. Reluctantly she looked up, then opened her eyes wide in surprise. Jamie had changed and was presumably dining out early. A dark, executive-style suit replaced the lightweight suit he wore about the clinic, his crisp white shirt looked new, and she would have sworn that the silver-grey tie was silk. Wanda was a lucky girl.

'Will I pass, Sister Scott?' His eyes were smiling at

her, and Linda relaxed. His ill humour had gone, though his remark still rankled.

'I was thinking how nice you looked,' she commented acidly, and he chuckled.

'Nice isn't much of a word, but it's better than nasty. Have you phoned him yet?' he asked, coming right into the room and perching on the corner of her desk.

Linda shuffled back from the desk a little, to give him more room, but to her consternation he merely eased himself a bit further on, and smiled down at her, as if they'd never crossed swords. She mistrusted that lazy smile. In fact, she mistrusted everything about him! It was when he was at his most charming and pleasant that he was at his most dangerous. His manner invited confidences, and for one terrible moment Linda was tempted to pour out all her troubles, tell him about Paul, beg him for help. . .

Instead she smiled sweetly. Being charming and attentive was part of his stock-in-trade. It was what psychiatrists were good at, and she really ought to have known better than to suppose he was actually interested in *her* problems. The poor man had enough problems brought to him by the patients.

'Is there something else you would like me to do before I go?' she asked, hoping he would take the hint.

'Is it clocking off time already? Yes, I suppose it is,' he agreed, glancing at the expensive-looking gold watch on his wrist. He had to peel back his cuff to see the watch and Linda caught a glimpse of dark hair on his arm, made more noticeable by the tanned skin. Evidently tanned all over.

He slid off the desk, frowning, and Linda wondered what was coming next. 'I shouldn't work too late, Linda, our days are long enough as it is. Hadn't you better telephone your man-friend?'

'Not from the Clinic, it wouldn't be right. I'll ring him when I leave. He can wait a few minutes, I should think,' Linda said tightly.

Jamie raised a brow fractionally, an irritating habit he had when he didn't believe her, and she bit her lower lip, mentally counting to ten again. She was going to do a lot of counting to ten here, she was sure of it!

'Luckily I answered the phone straight away,' he went on. 'He seemed a bit fraught.'

'Well, yes, he may have been. He usually is,' Linda said honestly.

'Is he an ex-patient, Linda?' Jamie didn't actually frown this time, but the frown was in his voice. Had she eaten the forbidden fruit? was the unasked question.

'No, I haven't—I mean, yes, he is, but not mine. I was never his nurse, if that was the question,' she hurried on, flustered.

'I'm glad to hear that. But——' He stopped, then shrugged. 'It's none of my business, but don't let him take over your life. He sounds the sort who will.'

That was too much, and Linda got up, banging her knee against the desk in her hurry. Wincing with pain, she hissed, 'I should have thought *you* were the sort of man who likes taking over people's lives, Dr Grainger! Paul isn't like that. He's sweet and vulnerable and—and he needs me,' she finished.

'He probably does—but do you need *him*?' He leaned towards her, his eyes questioning, and Linda almost told him she didn't need Paul but couldn't find a kind way to get rid of him. There it was again, that need to confide in someone, let someone else shoulder the burdens that were rightfully hers. It wouldn't do, and she must watch herself in future.

Despite what Jamie had seen—or thought he had seen—she and Paul weren't lovers, and as far as she was concerned, there was no question that they would ever be. Paul had seemed to accept that all she could offer was friendship, a shoulder to lean on, a helping hand along the way, and that had suited her. She wasn't in love with him, much as she liked him, and for her, there couldn't be sex without love.

Now, however, he was becoming truculent over this, and Linda foresaw trouble ahead. He was such a sensitive person that he would need very careful handling, and she wished he could be more like Jamie. It was difficult to imagine the debonair psychiatrist leaning on anybody!

Varied expressions chased themselves across her face, and Jamie's eyes narrowed. She could almost read *his* mind this time: she loved the man but has grown tired of him and doesn't have the guts to tell him. He's probably suicidal and she's making him ten times worse. Well, Paul *could* be, that was the awful part about it. If he wasn't handled right, who could say what he would do?

She let out her breath in a pent-up sigh, and looked about for her bag, remembering that she'd flung it into a corner. 'I'd better be getting along, as you say,' she said shakily. 'Tomorrow's another day. I——'

'Linda, look at me,' he commanded, but she refused to do so. Instead she picked up her bag and bent her head, scrabbling about in its capacious interior for her gold pen. It wouldn't do if she lost that.

'Linda.' Jamie spoke more softly this time, but there was an unmistakable order in that one word, and reluctantly she met his gaze. 'He isn't worth it, my dear. We do patients no service by trying to shoulder all their burdens. Let him stand on his own feet for a while. He might get to like it.'

'Yes, yes, he might. Well, he does. When you saw us, I was saying goodbye to him—I didn't know how long for at the time,' Linda rushed on, anxious for him to understand. 'He said he was going away. He needed to recharge his batteries. That suited me, so——' She shrugged helplessly. 'As far as I know, he's still away. He's an orphan, but his sister lives in Shoreham and I think he went there. Perhaps she's thrown him out!' Wearily she turned away, her groping fingers at last finding the gold pen. 'I'll be off now. Shall I see you tomorrow? Oh no, you're at a conference, aren't you?'

'Mm, just for a couple of days. Remember what I said about this man, Linda. Let him spread his wings, find his true self, solve his own problems. Then, when he comes back to you, he'll be his own man again. Remember, male pride is a delicate flower! Who knows, when he returns, he may shower you with roses and carry you off to the nearest church to legitimise your union. Isn't that worth waiting for?'

With a brief nod, he was gone, and Linda stared at the open doorway. If only he knew how wrong he was! She picked up the note of Paul's phone number and saw that the code was for Shoreham. At least he was with his sister, that was a bonus.

A fitful sun was trying to shine as she paused at the rear entrance to the Clinic, but Linda didn't really notice the sun, all she saw were Jamie Grainger's kind eyes, his infectious chuckle, his soothing words. A lump came into her throat, and, angry with herself, she crossed over to her car. Wallowing in self-pity did no one any good, and for a mental nurse to be like that on duty was totally indefensible. Psychiatric nursing was hard enough on the emotions as it was. Damn Paul, and damn Jamie Grainger!

There was no reply from the Shoreham number when Linda rang it immediately she got home, and it was with a faint feeling of unease that she replaced the receiver. Paul was probably all right and had gone out for a packet of cigarettes. He'd started smoking again, she'd noticed, after promising faithfully that he would give it up. Yes, that must be what it was, and perhaps his sister had gone out for the evening.

She tried again a few minutes later, then at half-hourly intervals, finally reaching him just after ten.

'Missed me, have you?' Paul's voice was bright and cheery, and Linda sent up a silent prayer of thankfulness.

'I may have done,' she admitted cautiously, and there was a silence at the other end. 'Paul? Are you still there?'

'Yes, I suppose so. Why don't you admit you missed me? I need you dreadfully, Linny.' His tone was wheedling, and she wondered quite why she'd ever agreed to be his friend. Too soft a heart was a minus factor sometimes.

I haven't had time to miss you,' she said honestly. 'I don't suppose you've really given me much of a thought, have you?' She put laughter into her voice.

'Perhaps—once or twice,' Paul admitted. 'Anyway, Janice says why don't you come down for the weekend? She'd love to meet you. Show me this paragon of virtue you're always on about, young Paul, she said, and I'll see if she's good enough to be your wife! That's Janice all over, rushing her fences,' he went on hurriedly, and Linda felt cold.

'I hope she realises we're just good friends, and that

marriage is definitely *not* on the agenda. Paul? You did tell her, didn't you?'

'No, I didn't. Why upset her? She's got plans for my future and apparently a capable wife is part of those plans, so why spoil it for her? *I* know you don't love me, but Janice won't understand that.'

'I don't love anyone, Paul, and that's all there is to it. If you want me to meet Janice, I'd be glad to, but you have to tell her the truth.'

'Yes, but——'

'You owe her the truth, Paul. It isn't fair to let her make plans for a wedding that won't take place,' Linda said firmly. That was *one* idea she had to nip in the bud! She wasn't sure it was a good idea to visit his sister, but it would be churlish to refuse. Janice might have more ideas on how to cope with Paul than she did. Relatives were always a mine of information, even when they didn't know they were being helpful. Yes, it would be as well to meet Janice.

'I'll tell her, then,' Paul said grumpily, then, before Linda could say more, her doorbell rang.

'Will you hang on for a moment until I see who's at the door?'

'Yes, all right. Probably a friend from the Clinic— that guy, I suppose? He didn't sound very pleased when I phoned.'

'Well, of course he wouldn't, Paul—that was the senior psychiatrist! We're not supposed to take personal calls. Hang on a jiffy.'

Linda flew to the door, then inched it open—to find the man himself just about to ring the bell for the second time.

'I didn't get you out of the bath, did I?' His smile was indulgent, and Linda flushed.

'No, not exactly. Come in, won't you?' She opened the door, but her expression was anything but inviting, she knew, and Jamie hesitated on the doorstep.

'Are you sure?'

'Yes, come in. I'm just on the phone, Doctor.' She raised her voice, hoping Paul would hear the word 'doctor', but when she picked up the receiver again, Paul had gone.

Carefully replacing the receiver on its cradle, Linda turned to Jamie, but couldn't speak. 'I—that was Paul. He——' Wearily she shook her head, then Jamie was beside her, his arms open invitingly.

Linda needed no second invitation. He clasped her to him, and thankfully she rested her head on his broad shoulder and closed her eyes. After the tumult of the day, Jamie's arms were a haven, and she asked nothing more.

CHAPTER THREE

AFTER a moment Linda pulled herself free, ashamed at losing control like that. What Jamie must be thinking of her, she could only surmise. 'I'm sorry, I——' She shook her head, then pinned a smile to her mouth. 'It's just that sometimes Paul——' She let the sentence trail off, knowing he would understand.

Jamie nodded. 'Don't take it too much to heart, Linda. I told you—let him find his own level, make his own decisions. He'll feel all the better for it.'

'Yes, but——'

'It's taking the first giant step that's so difficult,' he went on. 'Would you like me to have a word with him? No, that wouldn't help.' Jamie answered his own question, then smiled down at her, apparently dismissing Paul from his mind. 'I suddenly remembered—about the conference.'

'The "Psychiatry in the Nineties" conference? It sounds interesting—I'd love to hear about it. Would you like a cup of coffee?' Linda hurried on, glad of his company and surprised by the feeling.

The smile deepened. 'Thanks, I'd like that. Though I have to admit I've a favour to ask of you,' he added gently.

'Oh? If there's any way I can help, of course I will. Come into the sitting-room—it's a bit cramped, I'm afraid.' Linda led the way from the tiny hall into the cottage's main room, which still held most of the furniture she had inherited from her grandmother, together with the cottage. Seeing the room with the eye of a stranger, Linda realised that it was overcrowded, yet it was cosy too, and Jamie seemed at ease immediately.

'I'll just see to the coffee,' she called out, before disappearing into the only other room on the ground floor, an even tinier kitchen. Here there was room only for the cooker, a small table and a fridge. She often ate in the kitchen, but could hardly entertain her boss there! Humming happily, she filled the kettle, set a match to the gas, then put out a couple of mugs before going back to the sitting-room, wondering what it was Jamie needed her help with.

He'd fallen asleep! Surprised, Linda hovered in the doorway, anxious not to disturb him. He was sprawled in the chair, eyes closed, his head resting on her favourite cushion—the last thing her grandmother had embroidered.

Tears sprang to her eyes. She wanted to drink her fill, knowing this might be the only opportunity she had to see the psychiatrist at his most vulnerable. It was funny, but the antagonism she had felt for him right from the first had evaporated now. All she could see was a gentle, caring doctor, a man who set high standards for himself and expected—no, *demanded*, that others follow suit. How could she fault him for that?

Whatever relationship he and the mysterious Wanda had, he was discreet about it, brought no scandal either upon himself or the Clinic, and that was what mattered.

Jamie had discarded his dark suit jacket and hung it neatly across the back of the chair. He had loosened the silk tie Linda had been admiring earlier, and undone the top two buttons of his shirt. He looked so very much at home that sudden longing overcame her, and she went quietly back to the kitchen. She hummed quietly to herself as she got down the tin of biscuits which was part of the stock her mother had pressed upon her at the weekend. Good old Mum!

The kettle boiled and she made the coffee. Then, making as much noise as possible, she carried the mugs in on the tray, glad to see that Jamie was awake now. He rose at her noisy entrance, that slow, sensuous smile transforming his face, and quickly Linda looked away, concentrating on putting the tray down, a lock of hair hiding her expression from him.

'There we are—coffee and biscuits, sir!' she said brightly. 'My mother always insists on stocking me up with food whenever I go home!'

'Aha! So *that's* where you spent the weekend!' Their eyes met, and Linda saw that he was laughing at her.

They sat companionably together, drinking the coffee and eating her mother's home-baked biscuits. Their talk was desultory, yet there were no awkward silences, no sullen looks from her guest, such as she was used to from Paul. And, most blessed of all, she didn't need to hedge around difficult topics. Jamie was easy to talk to, naturally, because of his training, but it was more than that. They discovered quite a few interests in common.

'Did you see the first night of *Richard the Third*?' he asked, after finding out that her mother lived near Stratford-upon-Avon, and that they shared an interest in the theatre.

'Yes, I did. I was really impressed, though I'm sure King Richard wasn't as black as Shakespeare painted him!' she remarked, and Jamie nodded.

'No, that's true. Shakespeare rewrote history to suit the Tudors, that's the trouble. Ever since, schoolchildren have believed Shakespeare's view of people like Richard the Third, rather than the view historical evidence might present. I believe Richard murdered the Princes in the Tower, though,' Jamie added, with a mischievous twinkle, and Linda opened her mouth to protest.

'No! He——' Then she stopped, something in Jamie's eyes causing all thoughts of Richard the Third to leave her mind.

'I was just thinking how kissable your mouth looks,' he said easily, just as if they were discussing the weather. 'Perhaps we ought to get back to Shakespeare?' he suggested.

'Yes, perhaps we should. I—would you like more coffee?' For a moment Linda couldn't think straight, and would have been glad of the opportunity to dash into the kitchen to compose herself, but Jamie shook his head.

'No, thank you. I'd better be going—— Oh, about the conference.' He tapped the briefcase by his side, and Linda waited, still dazed. *I was just thinking how kissable your mouth looks. . .* She couldn't get his words out of her mind, and knew they would echo in her head long after he had gone. Unnerved by the intensity of his gaze, she ran a tongue over her lips in an unconsciously provocative gesture, and Jamie groaned.

'Shakespeare was a safer topic,' he murmured, then reached across for her. Knowing he was forbidden fruit, Linda nevertheless raised her face for his kiss, hardly believing that this was happening. *He belongs to Wanda!* her brain said sternly, but her heart waved her brain to silence, as her lips parted for Jamie's kiss.

When they broke apart, after what must have only been a few seconds, Linda was shaken and breathless, and knew she would feel the sweet pressure of his mouth on hers for the rest of the evening. Wonderingly, she gazed at him, pushing Wanda—and Paul—to the back of her mind for a moment.

Then reality intruded, and Jamie gazed down at her, his expression sombre. 'I apologise, Linda. I had no right. . .'

'No,' she agreed, shaking her head to try to clear it. 'There are others to consider,' she added, thinking of Wanda.

'Yes, we can't always have what we want in this life, can we? I'd better go.' He reached for his jacket, and Linda watched him, misery staring out of her eyes. Then she saw the briefcase.

'You wanted to tell me something—about the conference, I mean.'

'Yes, so I did,' he sighed. 'Actually, I wanted your help. I need one of my papers typed urgently and Nurse Craig told me you often type out your reports.'

'Yes, that's true. My mother insisted I take typing lessons when I left school—in case nursing wasn't the wonderful career I was certain it was,' she said, her voice edgy. He needed a casual typist, so he'd come to her!

'Never mind—I'd better go.' Jamie shrugged into the jacket, then fixed his tie, while Linda tried to avert her gaze, but could not. Whatever his feelings in the matter, she had enjoyed that kiss and wanted more—much more.

Ashamed of the intensity of her feelings, she said, 'Since you took the trouble to bring your work all the way out here, the least I can do is to type it for you! I'll just bring my typewriter down. It's lucky I have my own machine, isn't it?' she went on brightly. The nerve of the man! Perhaps the kiss was all part of the softening-up process!

No, that wasn't so, she acknowledged, as she carefully

carried the small, lightweight machine down the stairs. Jamie had been as carried away as she was, and he had enjoyed kissing her, she had seen that in his eyes.

She tried to make amends as she carried the machine through to the kitchen. 'I always type in here. I've got lazy, I'm afraid, I always type personal letters—my handwriting isn't anything to be proud of!' she laughed, but even to her, her voice sounded shrill, unnatural.

'Listen, Linda, it really doesn't matter,' Jamie began. 'I'll struggle to read my own writing. Please don't bother.' He put out a hand as if to restrain her, but she ignored it.

'That's all right, Doctor, it's no bother, really,' she assured him, her voice strained with the effort she was making. Whatever happened, she mustn't let him see how hurt she was, how much she had enjoyed that brief moment in his arms.

Without another word, he handed her the report and Linda began typing, her mind far away from what she was doing, and she made several mistakes, and had the embarrassment of having to start again. 'Sorry, I'm tired, I suppose,' she murmured, inserting a fresh sheet in the typewriter. 'I never asked you—do you want a carbon copy, or is the one enough?' She smiled up at him, but it was a cool, professional smile, and his lips tightened.

'No carbon, thank you. I'll sit down again, let you get on.' He sprawled on the rug in front of the hearth, his face averted, and she found she could gaze at him from time to time without disturbing the rhythm of her typing too much. She'd hurt him, but hadn't he hurt her? Her pain was the greater, she was sure of it. Wanda was welcome to him, that was all she could say!

At last the report, only a short one, was finished, and Linda carefully read it through, determined not to be blamed for typos. 'Yes, I think that's all right—do you want to read it? I may have misread something, you never know!' There was silence for a moment, then Jamie rolled over on the rug, taking his time about getting up, and her heart missed a beat. Whether he knew it or not, Dr Jamie Grainger was a very desirable man, and Sister Linda Scott most certainly desired him!

'Yes, perhaps I'd better.' He paused. 'Your friend Paul isn't coming home tonight, is he? I don't want to be here when he gets back, he might misconstrue my presence,' he added, with a wry smile.

'I'm sure he'd do nothing of the sort,' Linda said stiffly, knowing it was a lie. 'Paul isn't like that. He——'

'Is he gay, then? You surprise me.'

'Oh, no, far from it!' Linda protested.

'I see. Well, thank you for the report, Linda. I'm grateful.' Jamie had been reading it while they spoke of Paul, and now he stowed her typed copy carefully away in his briefcase. 'I'll be back on Thursday—the afternoon, most probably. I've a clinic at the General on Thursday morning and I'll go straight there. Dr Ahmed will be in charge, so nothing should go wrong.' With a brief smile, Jamie made his way out, not even waiting for her to accompany him to the door, and she sat at her typewriter, listening as the front door closed quietly behind him.

She sat there long after that too, long after she ought to have been in bed, simply staring into space, not seeing the flowered wallpaper in front of her, not seeing anything except a man she was beginning to care for. How ridiculous could you get?

* * *

'Go on, Sister, have another slice!' Mrs Salisbury beamed at Linda, as she handed round her birthday cake at the Clinic on Thursday.

'Well, I really shouldn't, but I will!' With alacrity, Linda accepted another slice of the delicious, light-textured sponge. 'You'll have to give me baking lessons, Mrs Salisbury. I'm afraid I rely on my old mum to provide me with home-made goodies!'

Alice Salisbury beamed all the more by the time the rest of the patients in the small group had finished praising her baking abilities. It was a clinic for the obsessive-compulsive patients, a group of people Linda particularly liked. They were ordinary folk, just like herself, and it served to prove, if proof was needed, that having a psychiatric disorder didn't mean madness, or being 'queer' or in any way different. The unpleasant and debilitating symptoms could attack anyone, from any background, and in the group she had patients who were housewives, one who ran her own successful business, another who was a retired teacher. This was the last group meeting for them, and the cake served a double purpose, a way of celebrating a birthday with friends, and a farewell to the Summerheath Clinic.

It was into this festive atmosphere that Paul barged, and Linda's eyes widened with dismay at seeing him in the doorway, smiling eagerly at her.

'Sorry! I didn't mean to break in, but——'

'I'll see you outside, Paul,' she said swiftly. 'Excuse me, ladies! Shan't be long.' Quickly she ushered Paul outside and closed the door firmly. 'I'm in the middle of a clinic—you really shouldn't have interrupted,' she said gently, and he gave her a disbelieving look.

'It seemed more of a party to me! I didn't think I was

interrupting anything, and I couldn't see anyone to ask,' Paul pointed out.

That was true, anyway. The receptionist had deserted her post for that crucial moment. 'Well, it *is* a party, in a way. It's the end of that particular group and we're celebrating a birthday as well,' Linda admitted.

'There you are, then! I didn't interrupt any dreadful confidences, did I? No, of course not. Aren't you going to kiss your Paul? You haven't seen me for—oh, let me see now——'

'No, Sister hasn't seen you for some time, but I suggest you greet each other *outside* working hours,' a stern voice broke in, and Linda closed her eyes in dismay. *He* wasn't due back for at least an hour!

Wanting Jamie to remember that Paul was an ex-patient, Linda swiftly made the introductions, even though she could feel the ice in the air. 'Dr Grainger, this is Paul Winterton. He's my lodger, as you're aware,' she added sharply.

'Ah, yes. How do you do, Mr Winterton? Did you enjoy the sights of Shoreham?' Jamie asked smoothly.

'Well, yes, thank you, I did.' A strangely subdued Paul accepted the hand the psychiatrist offered. 'I'm not exactly a lodger, you know. Linda and I are——'

'Whatever relationship you have with my day patient sister, it isn't my concern,' Jamie interposed, while a fuming Linda stood there, and could do nothing. Whatever she said, Jamie wouldn't believe her.

'No, of course not, Doctor,' Paul said obediently. 'I've had clinical depression rather badly, so I hope you won't be *too* hard on me,' he added, with an apologetic smile. 'I was an in-patient at the Baxter, you know, and Linda—Sister Scott, that is—was extremely helpful to me. She——'

'I'm delighted to hear that, but I've got rather a busy afternoon, Mr Winterton. Perhaps you'll excuse me.' Without another word, Jamie strode off, and Linda turned her reproachful gaze on Paul.

'That's *all* I need! I'm already in his bad books,' she muttered crossly, forgetting for a moment that she had to watch every word.

'That's not my fault!' Paul flared up. 'If you don't want me any more, why not say so? Calling me your lodger when that man must know we're lovers!' His voice rose, and Linda's face burned with shame. Jamie wasn't that far along the corridor. He might have heard, and certainly Nurse Craig must have done, for she materialised out of nowhere, and was eyeing them with avid curiosity.

Now she came across to them, and in a way Linda was glad. Muriel Craig could deal with Paul while she got back to her patients. 'Is everything all right, Sister? Hello, I haven't seen you here before.' With a brisk smile, the nurse turned to Paul, and he responded accordingly.

'I used to be a patient at the Baxter, Staff,' he said eagerly. 'Linda worked there, you know, and——'

'Yes, so she did. Well, you come along and tell me all about it. I'll get you a cup of tea, shall I? Sister Scott has to get back to her patients or they'll be running riot!' Gently but firmly Nurse Craig led the unresisting Paul away, and Linda breathed a sigh of relief.

'Sorry, ladies,' she murmured, as she rejoined her group. From the sharp looks she received, she realised they must have heard Paul's outburst, but it couldn't be helped. Surely they realised that doctors and nurses had personal problems too?

'We're glad you're back, Sister, because, as it's our

last time here, we've got a little surprise for you.' Proudly, Mrs Salisbury held out a gift-wrapped package, and, wonderingly, Linda took it.

Carefully she felt all around it, amid giggles from some of the ladies. 'I can't tell what it is—I shall have to open it, shan't I?' She unwrapped three layers of paper, hoping the patients hadn't gone to any expense for her. She was merely doing her duty, after all, and it was her predecessor who had got that particular group underway. Nestling inside the last layer of wrapping paper was a pretty cameo necklet with matching earrings. 'Oh, ladies! It's lovely. Thank you—but you shouldn't. I haven't been here more than a few days!'

'No, that's true,' one of the others interposed, 'but you're a great improvement on the last sister, efficient though she was, and we've grown fond of you. Haven't we, girls?' She turned to the others for support, and there were murmurs of assent.

'Three cheers for Sister Scott!' Mrs Salisbury said suddenly, and Linda had to stand there while they cheered her. Overcome with gratitude though she was, she was afraid the noise might bring Jamie back, and he might not appreciate the fuss the ladies were making of her. At the moment, she wasn't his favourite person!

Jamie paused, his eyes hooded so that Linda couldn't read his expression. 'I don't like to spoil your pleasure in what was an unsolicited gift, Linda, but there *are* rules about accepting gifts from patients.'

'Yes, I know,' Linda said warily, 'there were at the Baxter, but that was gifts from in-patients, particularly the elderly, whose relatives might think nurses had been influencing them, but surely——'

'A rule is a rule, Linda. I'm sorry.' Jamie ran long

fingers through his unruly hair, and her eyes followed the gesture. 'It's my fault, I should have made it clear. Perhaps a notice put up in the Clinic might be a good idea? What do you think?'

'I didn't think I was supposed to have any ideas!' Linda snapped, aware that she was being unfair. Jamie was only pointing out something she'd known all along— that psychiatric nurses, certainly *trained* psychiatric nurses, didn't accept presents from patients. It was an unwritten rule, certainly, but one she had always obeyed until today. Yet how could she have done otherwise? No, she felt Jamie was cross with her over Paul, and the gift was just the excuse he needed to reprimand her.

'I'll pretend I didn't hear that remark,' he said softly, and Linda glanced away.

'I'm sorry, Jamie, really I am. I'm sorry about Paul as well, but I wasn't to know he'd come breezing in like that!'

'No, that's true, but——' He sat down, the swivel chair moving slightly as he did so. 'Do sit down, Linda. You look like a naughty schoolgirl waiting to be caned!' He grinned at her, that lazy grin again, and, weak-kneed, Linda did as she was told.

'I *feel* like a naughty schoolgirl,' she admitted, carefully avoiding his eyes. 'Have I to give back the cameo? They'll be dreadfully hurt.'

'No, no, I didn't mean you to. Keep it. They're finished with the Clinic—for now, anyway. One of them will be back next year with similar symptoms, though,' he added broodingly. 'She hasn't made the progress the others have, though she's undoubtedly licked the problem this time.'

Linda knew which patient he meant, the retired teacher who had to perform certain rituals every day, such as washing her hands fourteen times after using the lavatory, and vigorously scrubbing the bath and basin after each hand-washing because she feared she was leaving germs everywhere and killing people. It wasn't an uncommon problem, but Linda was determined the patient would remain well.

'That's what I wanted to speak to you about, Jamie—the follow-up clinic. Can I have one as well?'

'Why, yes, if you'd like to. Have you the time?' He seemed genuinely interested in her suggestion, and Linda breathed a sigh of relief. At least when they were discussing patient care they weren't at each other's throats! The problem of Paul Winterton was shelved for the moment as Linda enlarged on her suggestions, and it was after six by the time she emerged from Jamie's office, well pleased with her success. Her smile faded as a figure rose from a bench in the waiting-room. Paul was still there!

She wasn't quick enough to alter her expression, and Paul's eyes narrowed. They were as dark as Jamie's were light, and unfathomable. She never knew *what* Paul was thinking, though she had a pretty good idea at the moment!

'Sorry, did I interrupt a meeting?' Paul laughed lightly, but there was no humour behind it, and one of Jamie's brows flicked upward.

'No, Sister Scott and I were finished, thank you. How about a coffee?' The invitation was extended to them both, but Paul refused.

'Thanks, but we really ought to get back. We haven't seen each other for several days—you know how it is?'

'I'll see you tomorrow, Dr Grainger,' Linda said levelly, her eyes willing him to understand how difficult it was.

'Yes, please be prompt—Fridays are always busy.' Jamie's voice was curt, and Linda turned away, sick at heart. Something must be done about Paul. He had leaned on her for long enough. Jamie must be made to see that there was nothing between them.

Remember Wanda, she told herself, as she hurried to the locker-room. Whatever Jamie believes about you and Paul, it doesn't matter in the long run—*he's* already spoken for.

Paul had brought his own car, an ancient sports car, and Linda was free to follow the drift of her own thoughts as she headed her car in the direction of the cottage. Paul was ahead, and she hung back, letting another couple of cars overtake her. She wanted him to be out of her sight while she thought the matter through. She'd been wrong to let him stay while he 'sorted myself out', as he put it. He should have sorted out his problems by now, and Jamie was right in that respect—Paul wouldn't stand on his own feet all the while she and others like her propped him up. Perhaps the coming weekend visiting his sister would be useful.

She was in the Clinic very early the next morning, glad to get away from the atmosphere at her cottage. Paul hadn't taken kindly to being told to keep away from the Clinic, and had almost accused her of being in love with Jamie Grainger. Almost, but not quite. At the last moment, he had drawn back, perhaps appalled by the fury in her eyes. She had accepted his apology, but with his mind full of suspicions it wasn't the time to ask him to leave. After the weekend, or perhaps during it would be better. It depended on what sort of relationship his sister had with Paul.

'Friday—call for Mrs Skilton, then agoraphobic clinic. Free after lunch,' Linda read aloud from her diary, then closed it with a snap. It was only just after eight and only the nurses from the in-patient unit were about. Idly, she got up and crossed to the window. From there, she had an excellent view of the extensive gardens at the front of the Clinic. Round by the side was the car park, and as she watched, a long, sleek Jaguar came smoothly up the drive and turned into the car park.

Hoping Jamie hadn't seen her, Linda turned away and was busy typing a report when he appeared in the doorway, that little smile hovering about his mouth. Evidently he was in a better mood, and she wondered whether Wanda was responsible for that.

'You're an early bird, Linda. Thank you for typing my report, by the way. I never thanked you properly, did I?' he murmured, coming right into the office.

'You said thank you, and it wasn't much. One and a quarter sheets of A4 was hardly a great labour!'

'No, perhaps not,' he agreed softly, then, before she was aware of his intention, he dropped a light kiss on her brow. 'Thank you, anyway. Everything all right with the boyfriend?'

'What? Oh, yes, thank you.' If her voice sounded unnatural, who could expect otherwise? Jamie was full of contradictions, and she never knew which way to take him. 'Paul isn't my boyfriend!' she exploded, suddenly recalling what he'd said. That kiss had thrown her, as usual!

'Isn't he? He seems to think so,' Jamie pointed out, his eyes sad. 'If there's nothing between you, then now might be the time to get rid of him. If he *is* only a lodger——'

'He is,' she said tightly, then began typing again, letting Jamie see that the matter was closed. He had no right to interfere in her private life, and it was evident that he didn't believe her, anyway.

Mrs Skilton was the main task for the day, but Linda had an ally this time—Jamie decided to accompany her when she went to fetch the patient for the agoraphobic clinic. To her surprise, he hadn't agreed that the psychologist be called in again. He considered it would merely reinforce Mrs Skilton's belief that she was getting worse and needed to be admitted.

They went in Jamie's car, and she relaxed on the way there, closing her eyes briefly. During the night, she'd heard Paul pacing up and down the cottage, first in his bedroom, then going noisily downstairs before clattering about in the kitchen making coffee and leaving the place untidy.

She sighed, hardly aware of the fact, and felt Jamie's disapproval coming across in waves. 'Sorry, I had a disturbed night,' she said quietly, then blushed, believing he might misconstrue the remark.

'So did I,' he said equably, and she was left wondering what he meant. They were at Mrs Skilton's now and she had no opportunity to probe, not that she wanted to, of course. . .

Gwen Skilton was determined not to attend the Clinic, and nothing either of them could say would change her mind. Once or twice she had seemed about to tell them something, then had withdrawn again. Clearly she had regressed further than Jamie had thought, and the way back would be long and hard.

They left, after Linda had promised to call again on Monday. It could be that the patient would be more open about her problem if Linda saw her alone.

As soon as she could, Linda was determined to have a

word with the community psychiatric nurse, who supported people like Mrs Skilton at home. They were the key workers, and if the CPN had fixed ideas on how best to cope, she felt she couldn't interfere. Mrs Skilton was a lady who needed one person to whom she could relate, and that one person must have all the time in the world to spend with her.

She wrestled with the problem on the drive back. If only she herself had more time! It might mean working some weekends, though the strain of working with people like that was greater than lay people realised. It was emotionally as well as physically draining, and with Paul to cope with, in addition, it might prove too much.

'How is he?' They were nearly back at the Clinic before Jamie spoke, and Linda started, wondering who they were talking about for a moment.

'He? Do you mean Paul? He's all right, I suppose. He was in bed when I left,' she added without thinking, then nibbled her lower lip, suddenly realising what she'd said.

'Hasn't he got a job?' Jamie's tone dripped ice, and she immediately flew to Paul's defence.

'Of course he has! He's a writer. He doesn't sit at home living on State handouts, if that's what you're implying! He's going through writers' block at the moment. That's partly why he went to stay with his sister, he thought a change of scenery would do him good,' she rushed on, but Jamie didn't comment.

It was nearly time to leave for the weekend before she and Jamie were alone again as Fridays were always busy, and the agoraphobic clinic took up most of the morning.

She couldn't stop for lunch, not if she was to get through the paperwork and make a few phone calls. Jamie liked the Clinic to keep in touch with patients who had been discharged, and Friday afternoon was a good time to do that, he felt. It was long past one o'clock before she had time to pop into the snack bar attached to the canteen and buy a sandwich. Jamie was there, as luck would have it, but she tried to pretend she hadn't seen him. She really didn't want to discuss Paul again, and Jamie seemed unable to keep off the subject.

She had barely sat down again at her desk when the psychiatrist followed her. He hovered in the doorway as if uncertain of his welcome, and the glance she gave him was cool. 'May I come in, Sister? Or am I still in your bad books for criticising your loved one?' he added, not waiting for an invitation. To her consternation, he sat beside her, and she had to force a smile to her mouth.

'You aren't in my bad books, Doctor—why should you be? You're entitled to your opinion, no matter how wrong that might be,' she said stiffly, then was disconcerted to hear him chuckle.

'Of course I'm wrong. Tell me how wrong I am,' he suggested, but Linda refused to say any more, merely concentrated on her sandwich.

Jamie shrugged, then bit into an apple, his amused gaze still on her. She could feel her face heating, and blamed it on the hot day. It was the sort of day for wearing a sundress, and Nurse Craig was wearing one, but Linda felt it wouldn't be professional, certainly not for a sister, so she had opted for a cool cotton top and a simple flared skirt in beige. Being pale, she didn't tan, and realised belatedly that the colour beige did nothing for her. She probably looked as washed-out as she felt! Oh, well, no doubt Jamie didn't care too much what she looked like as long as she was tidy and respectably dressed.

Wondering what the elusive Wanda looked like, Linda

was about to comment on the weather when Jamie forestalled her. 'Going home for the weekend, Linda? I shall picture you strolling by the Avon in the sunshine!'

She shook her head, a strand of her fine blonde hair brushing against his arm as she did so. 'No, I'm not. I——' she began, meaning to tell him about Paul's sister.

'Does that mean you're free tomorrow?' Jamie's gaze was quizzical.

'Free? Well, I——'

'Good—it's just the weather for a picnic, wouldn't you agree?' he went on easily, and Linda didn't know what to say.

'Well, yes, it *would* be nice, but I'm sorry, really I am, but it just isn't possible,' she said reluctantly.

'You told me Paul's only a lodger,' Jamie pointed out calmly. 'Therefore he can't possibly object to his land-lady spending part of her day off with friends. He hasn't the right—or has he, Linda?'

There was a waiting silence and Linda, who wasn't usually stuck for words, simply couldn't think of the right ones. 'No, he hasn't the right,' she said at last, 'but he's going to spend the weekend with his sister in Shoreham, and I'm going with him.'

'I see. That's a pity, you might have enjoyed the picnic.'

'Yes, yes, I would have.'

'There was someone I wanted you to meet, but perhaps another time,' he said cheerfully, as if her refusal meant nothing. He finished the apple, then with a wave he was gone, leaving Linda to stare into a bleak future, and an even bleaker weekend. She had no idea who it was Jamie had wanted her to meet, but was rather afraid it was Wanda. She certainly wasn't in any hurry to meet *her*!

★　★　★

Mrs Skilton appeared not to be at home when Linda called on her on Monday. Since she never went out, she must be hiding somewhere in the house, lonely and afraid. To try to trick her by going away and then creeping around the back of the house would be unethical, and might do more harm than good. Yet somehow she must be made to open the door—but how?

Hating to give up and leave the patient more time to dwell on her fears, Linda called through the letterbox, and at last was rewarded when a muffled voice spoke to her. 'Is that you, Sister? I thought it was those double-glazing people again! They keep coming, you know. Never leave us alone,' Mrs Skilton complained through the letterbox, and Linda tried to reassure her.

'Yes, it's me again! I'm awfully dry—do you suppose I could have a cup of tea before I go back? I've missed my canteen break,' she added craftily, and the door was immediately opened a crack to enable Mrs Skilton to peer out at her.

'Oh, it *is* you, dear. Come in, I'll just pop the kettle on.' She left the door ajar, and Linda ventured in, the heat in the house hitting her. All the windows were closed, she realised, as she followed Mrs Skilton into the kitchen. On her previous visit it hadn't seemed so stifling.

'It's very hot in here, Mrs Skilton—shall I open a window?' she suggested, her eyes on the patient, who whirled round, a look of horror on her face.

'Oh, no! No, don't do that, Sister. I—I like it warm. I feel the cold dreadful, that I do,' she hurried on. 'Just you sit there and rest and I'll have the tea made in a jiffy. My husband's out.'

'Is he? Has he gone anywhere special?' Linda kicked off her sandals, undid the top button of her blouse and slipped her jacket off. Even so, the heat was almost unbearable, and the room smelled faintly of cats.

'He's gone to the hospital—the General, you know. Got an outpatient appointment again.'

'What a pity you couldn't have gone with him. He would have been glad of company, surely?' Linda suggested, wondering whether his appointments had some bearing on the severity of his wife's condition.

'If I could go out, of course I'd go with him. It's my place,' Mrs Skilton said firmly. 'There, I'll just warm the pot. The kettle won't be long. Make yourself at home, Sister,' she invited, and Linda chuckled.

'I already have, I'm afraid! Have you any pets? I thought I saw a cat in the garden.'

'Oh, yes, three—Timmo, Suki and Jason! Little devils, they are. Like their comfort, cats. I'll see if any of them are about.' She left the room, returning a few moments later with a large marmalade-coloured cat. 'This is Suki, dear. Say hello to the nice nurse; then, Suki!'

The cat totally ignored Linda, even when she stroked it, and she pulled a wry face. 'Evidently Suki doesn't like me. We could do with a cat—or a dog—at the Clinic, I thought. Patients often respond to animals even when they don't to human beings.' She waited for Mrs Skilton's reaction.

'Yes, I suppose they do. Still, none of them are really bad, are they? Not like me, I mean. Not at day patients. When I was an in-patient, now, that was different. But I'm not bad enough yet, am I? Dr Grainger doesn't think so, does he?' she went on, setting the cat down.

'Dr Grainger feels it's better for ladies like yourself to be treated at home, or in a day patient situation,' Linda explained. 'You gain nothing by going to hospital, Mrs

Skilton—you need more treatment than you're getting, though,' she added, and waited.

The reaction was as she had expected. Mrs Skilton came across and clutched her arm, oblivious to the kettle whistling away. 'Oh, I do, Sister! I do need help. Only my hubby, he doesn't always understand. If I could come into hospital, even for a few days, he'd have to realise I'm ill, wouldn't he? Then there's my daughter— she left home when she was a girl. She's married now and she visits now and again, but *she* doesn't think I'm ill, and I am, Sister, aren't I?' Her deep-set eyes pleaded for understanding, and Linda comforted her as best she could, letting the woman rest her head on her shoulder.

'It *is* an illness, yes,' she agreed, 'and you do need help, but we can beat this dreadful disability together— while you stay in your home or attend the Clinic. Isn't that better? I'll get the case-worker to have a word with your husband about it. Perhaps he doesn't fully under-stand the nature of agoraphobia. Maybe he thinks you can beat it by yourself—a lot of people believe that the person with a phobia can 'pull themselves together', but that isn't so easy,' Linda pointed out.

Mrs Skilton sighed. 'If you think that's best, Sister— but if you was to take me away into hospital, they'd both know I was ill, wouldn't they? I'll just make the tea.' She busied herself with the teapot, while Linda thought about the problem.

A hospital admission really wasn't the answer for this woman. She had been an in-patient before. True, she had been helped over her problem, but now the symp-toms had come back, only worse this time. The home environment clearly wasn't ideal, with husband and daughter presumably telling her to pull herself together, but since the environment couldn't be changed it was best for the patient to remain at home and learn to cope there.

They drank their tea in a companionable silence, and the cat even ventured back into the room, eyeing Linda in a more friendly fashion this time, and consenting to be petted. 'I really wish we could have Suki at the Clinic,' Linda said with a smile, as she prepared to leave. She hadn't mentioned the agoraphobic clinic, and gradually the tenseness had left her hostess. Evidently she had expected to be cajoled into attending, but that wasn't Linda's way. A little tender loving care was called for here!

'But cats don't travel well, you know, though she loves company! Don't you, my darling?' Mrs Skilton stroked Suki, who began to purr, at the same time treating Linda to such a disdainful look that she laughed.

'Take care of yourself, my dear. When would you like me to call again?' she asked as they stood on the doorstep, the patient refusing to venture any further.

'Oh, any time, Sister, any time at all. What about tomorrow? You could have another cup of tea!' Mrs Skilton beamed, and Linda mentally rearranged her programme for the following day.

As she drove slowly back to the Clinic, she reflected that Jamie wouldn't like her interfering in what was probably no longer going to be her concern, but she liked Mrs Skilton and genuinely felt she could help. The overworked CPN probably wouldn't object, but Dr Jamie Grainger was another matter!

He wasn't there when she returned to the Clinic, and Nurse Craig told her he had had to leave urgently. 'Had bad news, I think. Something personal, Sister.' Nurse Craig lowered her voice confidentially, and Linda wondered what was coming next. 'It was Wanda who phoned him. You know about Wanda, I suppose?' she went on, and Linda was quick to say she did.

'Yes, if Wanda rang, then of course he would have to hurry away,' she said, with a smile. 'And I must hurry into my next clinic, Staff. Let me know if Dr Grainger returns, will you?'

Clearly disappointed that Linda knew all about Wanda and that she wouldn't have the pleasure of telling her, Nurse Craig departed, and Linda forced a bright smile to her face as she prepared for her next group of patients.

'You know about Wanda, I suppose?' Well, yes, she was beginning to.

CHAPTER FOUR

IT WAS nearly five before Jamie returned to the Clinic, by which time Linda's head was a-buzz with all sorts of theories about Wanda. Obviously he loved the woman—he must do, to run to her the moment she called for help. Perhaps she, too, was an ex-patient, someone who desperately needed his guidance and kindness. Linda tried hard not to be jealous of the unknown Wanda, but it wasn't easy. Yet why should she care about the woman in his life? She valued her independence above all, and if Wanda was a dependent sort of woman she ought to feel sorry for her.

Yet the memory of that brief kiss from Jamie *would* keep coming back at the most inconvenient times, if indeed it had ever been away. Sighing a little, she began to make out her schedule for the following day, remembering to find a niche somewhere for Gwen Skilton. She'd tried, without success, to contact the CPN, and she couldn't bother Jamie, not now when he was troubled about his lady-friend.

'Ah, still here, Sister?' Jamie hovered in the doorway, his mouth smiling at her even though his eyes stayed cool and watchful.

'Yes, still here!' Linda said pleasantly, then bent her head to her work, not wanting her pleasure in his company to show.

Jamie put down his briefcase, then yawned, but she obstinately refused to look up. 'You sound tired—shall

61

I get you a cool drink? Or I'll put the kettle on, if you like?' she offered, still frowning over her diary.

There was silence, and Linda felt bound to glance up now—to see him eyeing her in amusement. 'Tea would be most welcome, thank you, Sister,' he said equably, then pulled out the chair opposite her desk and eased himself into it, wincing a little.

'Had a rough day?' Linda hadn't meant to ask, didn't want him to think she was prying, but longing overcame her. He looked so weary, so much in need of a willing ear or a shoulder to weep on, that she almost forgot their professional relationship and offered one!

He passed a hand across his eyes. 'Yes, it was rather. I had to see an old friend, then I did a couple of domiciliaries on the way back. One of them has an acute anxiety state and her GP's worried about her. He thinks she would be better as an in-patient, but I try to avoid that whenever possible. Go and make the tea, and think about the problem—I shall expect a solution by the time you come back!' he joked, and Linda pulled a face before doing as she was bid.

When she returned, Jamie was sitting at her desk busily writing. He glanced up and smiled, but it was a professional smile, those light eyes giving nothing away. The sort of smile he reserves for patients, Linda thought resentfully, but tried not to show it. After all, she was only his day patient sister, not a personal friend. She couldn't expect him to confide in her. Didn't *she* keep her personal problems to herself? Yet in such a caring environment it was sad that the two of them couldn't share their worries, their sadnesses as well as their happy times.

'You're deep in thought, Sister. What sort of day have *you* had? Tell me,' Jamie commanded, leaning back in her chair, while she perched on the edge of the one he had vacated.

'I sat in on the interview with a new patient, Miss Anstey. You saw her on a home visit a couple of weeks ago. She seemed quite well, apart from the obsessional thoughts,' Linda went on, and Jamie shrugged.

'Yes, on the surface she is. I suppose, compared with some people, she's very well. She copes with her full-time job—she's at the Bank in the High Street, she goes out and about, meeting people. Got quite a few friends, as well. It was one of the friends who alerted the GP.'

'And?'

'She's got so-called 'smiling' depression as well. They feel they must smile and sing through all difficulties, yet underneath they're really quite depressed. They carry on as if nothing was wrong, all the while bottling up their great inner sadness, and they're some of the hardest to reach. They've grown cunning and will be most indignant if anyone suggests they're depressed. They solve their own problems, and sometimes the only solution they can see is to end it all.'

'Beachy Head,' Linda said succinctly, and Jamie raised a brow.

'You seem to have an obsession with Beachy Head! I told you, it generally isn't local people who leap off the edge. Anyway, Lavinia Anstey isn't going to do that— I'd stake my pension on it. No, she'll go through life smiling and joking, though all the while her heart's breaking. No one understands that type of person, that's the trouble. She's lucky she's got at least one perceptive friend,' he went on, and they spent more time than Linda realised discussing the woman and depression generally.

Then Jamie glanced at his watch and swore. 'I should

have been home by now—I promised to be back by six.'
He rose, towering over her, and Linda carefully composed her face into what she hoped was a professional mask. Who was it he had promised? she wondered, as she gathered her notes and diary for the following day.

'Oh, I nearly forgot—but it doesn't matter,' she went on quickly, remembering Mrs Skilton.

'If it has to do with patients, Sister Scott, then it *does* matter.' Jamie's voice was soft, but there was a note of reproach in it.

'Yes, of course it does. It's about Mrs Skilton, but I didn't want to worry you with it tonight—not after you've had—after you've seen your friend, I mean,' Linda blundered on, and the atmosphere grew distinctly chillier.

Jamie gazed at her thoughtfully for a moment. 'Just because I took time off to see a friend, it doesn't mean I've pushed the patients to the back of my mind,' he said coldly.

'No, of course not, but I thought—with you hurrying away to see Wanda, that——'

'It was Wanda I wanted you to meet at the weekend,' he broke in. 'Did you enjoy your weekend, by the way? You were going to Shoreham, I seem to remember—to meet your young man's family,' he added pointedly.

'Please don't refer to Paul as my young man, Doctor,' Linda said with as much dignity as she could muster. 'He isn't, he's simply a friend and——'

'Just like Wanda, perhaps?' Before Linda could comment on *that*, he'd turned away and was picking up his briefcase, obviously keen to go home where perhaps Wanda was awaiting him.

His mention of the weekend brought the whole horrible episode home to her, and she wondered whether

Paul would be at the cottage when she got back. At the weekend, they'd had one whole grandaddy of a row, all four of them—Paul, Janice and her husband and Linda herself. Thanks to Paul's fertile imagination and half-truths, his sister had thrown her arms around Linda and welcomed her as a future sister-in-law!

It took a lot of tact and diplomacy to ensure that Janice understood: she and Paul were not in love, were not engaged, and had no intention of ever having a love affair, let alone marrying. Tact and diplomacy hadn't suited Paul, though, and Linda had lost her temper with him, his sister rushing to his aid like a she-bear, and the weekend had ended rather abruptly on Saturday evening!

Paul wasn't there when she got home, and Linda guiltily hoped that he wouldn't return, but supposed he would amble back eventually, expecting her to forgive him. If he came back for no other reason, he would do so to collect the manuscript of the mystery novel she was typing for him.

But there was still no sign of him by Friday morning and Linda hoped she could look forward to a peaceful weekend. Just for a change, she decided she would wear a summery dress for work, and chose her favourite, a loose-fitting dress in various shades of pink and violet. That would certainly stand out in a crowd! she thought in wry amusement. Whether Dr Grainger would approve was another matter. He had been rather preoccupied lately, brooding even, and Linda felt that was unlike him. It must be, because Nurse Craig had commented on it, and muttered darkly that it must be because Wanda wasn't too well.

Well, blow Wanda! Whoever she was, she had no right to upset the normally equable Jamie like that. Linda might have thought the woman was a relative, the

way Jamie hurried to her aid, but he'd said she was just
a friend—just like you and Paul, he'd added. Briefly, it
occurred to her that Wanda was his ex-wife, but since
she could hardly ask, that theory remained unproved.

She opened the windows of her car as she moved out
into the lane which ran alongside the six small cottages.
Then she had to put her foot hard on the brake as a
figure materialised out of the hedge that surrounded the
cottages, and waved her down. She drew into the side of
the lane and peered out at the young, very pregnant
woman.

'Thank goodness you stopped!' the woman panted.
'I've seen your car before—Mum lives at Number One
and she says you're a nurse! Could you come? She's lying
at the bottom of the stairs and I can't move her, not like
I am.' She patted her ample abdomen.

'Of course you can't! Here, get in the back and I'll
turn in the layby.' Linda held open the rear door and the
woman eased herself in.

'Thanks! I think she's broken something, she's that
grizzly,' she said, and Linda turned the car as quickly as
she could and headed back towards the cottages.

'I haven't seen you before,' Linda said, as they backed
into the lane. 'And I haven't met your mother—how did
she know I was a nurse?'

'Village grapevine. Very well supplied, that grapevine.
There's that old chap in Number Two, he's always to be
found a-gossiping away, talking to this one and that,' the
woman laughed. 'There isn't anything going on in the
area that he don't know about!'

She indicated that Linda should go into the cottage,
and Linda found a woman at the foot of the stairs, sitting
up and holding her head. Her face cleared when she saw
Linda, and she even managed a wan smile. 'Good thing

my girl caught you before you was off to that clinic, Sister,' she said, then winced as she felt her head. 'My head do ache so—can you give me summat?' she pleaded, but Linda shook her head.

'Not if you've broken anything, I can't. Where do you hurt—is it just your head?'

The woman, Mrs Honeysett, seemed to have sprained her ankle, and after a gentle examination, Linda decided nothing was broken, but as she had hit her head on the way down and still felt dizzy, a hospital investigation was advisable. 'I'll call an ambulance, I think. I could take you to the General in my car, but I think a stretcher might be more comfortable.'

The General decided to admit Mrs Honeysett for the night, and after she had seen her safely to bed, leaving her daughter with her, Linda belatedly remembered the Clinic. Of course, it was never far from her mind, and she had meant to phone the minute she arrived at the hospital, but it had completely slipped her mind. Jamie would be sending out a search party for her!

Then there was Gwen Skilton patiently waiting for a visit, and perhaps this might be the occasion when she had plucked up enough courage to come to the agoraphobic clinic! Wearily Linda pushed back her hair, her pale face already pink with exertion. It was warmer than ever, and all she really wanted to do was find somewhere cool to lie down—perhaps that swimming pool of Dr Grainger's! Yes, Dr Grainger, she must ring the Clinic. She could at least do *that*.

The receptionist put her straight through to Jamie, despite her protests that she only wanted to leave a message, and, seconds later, a curt voice was demanding to know where she had been.

'Do you realise that Mrs Skilton was waiting for you?'

he began, before Linda could get a word in. 'I nearly got her to the Clinic—if you'd been there, I might have succeeded!'

'I'm very sorry about that, Doctor,' Linda said coldly, 'but there was an emergency here and I had to help.'

'An emergency! I suppose it was that fool Winterton again? When will you learn not to keep running after him!' he barked, and Linda held on to her temper with difficulty.

'I don't know where Paul is, Doctor. The emergency was one of my neighbours—I'm at the General with her now. I'm sorry I didn't phone before, but I knew you'd understand,' she said sweetly, and there was silence at the other end.

If she thought Jamie might apologise, she was to be disappointed. 'I see,' was all he said. 'May we expect you at the Clinic at all today?'

'I'm on my way there now. I'm too late for the agoraphobics, but I can still help with the relaxation classes, if that's all right with you?' Really, the man was impossible! Here she was, doing her Good Samaritan act, and still that wasn't right!

'No, your clinics have been taken care of. Muriel Craig's doing the relaxations—she's just about to start, as a matter of fact. It would be a pity to disturb her.'

'Yes, it would,' Linda agreed, a lump in her throat.

'You sound in need of a little tender loving care yourself, Sister. Where are you exactly?' Jamie demanded.

'I'm in the main foyer. I——'

'Stay where you are,' he broke in curtly. 'I'll be along in about twenty minutes.' With that he put the receiver down, and Linda was left staring into space.

Why was he coming to the hospital? Didn't he believe

her story about her neighbour? It sounded very much as though he didn't! Hot tears sprang to the backs of her eyes as she walked slowly to the rows of plastic chairs and prepared to wait for her chief. Just when their relationship was getting on a better footing, this had to happen. The man was just as fault-finding as ever, and she didn't know how she was to bear it!

He was at the General well within the twenty minutes, and Linda glanced up warily as he came briskly through the swing doors and looked about him, a frown already beginning.

Let him frown! Childish though it was, she refused to acknowledge that she'd seen him, and watched as he searched the main foyer, before finally noticing her over by the tea-bar where she had sought refuge and the comfort that a cup of tea brought.

'Ah, there you are!' Jamie strode across to her, and she rose politely, tea cup clutched defensively to her chest. A smile tugged at the corners of his firm mouth, and Linda felt ashamed at her pettiness. Yet again he had made her feel insignificant. Well, she wasn't!

'Temper, temper, Sister Scott,' Jamie chided gently. 'I'll have a cup as well. Oh, and a packet of crisps, please.' With that, he sat down at the chair she had vacated, leaving a fuming Linda to buy his tea and crisps.

'Here we are, Doctor.' Carefully she placed the cup in front of him, then, with a surprised glance, gave him the crisps. 'I wouldn't have thought you'd eat junk food.'

Stowing the crisps away in his pocket, Jamie smiled up at her. 'Sit down, Sister Scott. Rest your little legs,' he added, which did nothing for Linda's ire.

'Thank you, I will. Why can't you buy crisps at the

Clinic? They had some in the canteen yesterday, I saw them.'

'Because I'm not going back to the Clinic just yet. And the crisps aren't for me, they're for a friend. As you say, I don't eat that sort of thing. Nibbling is a bad habit, Sister,' he said gently, and Linda nodded.

'Yes, but I'm afraid I do it! I like crisps, but at the moment I'm on another diet, so I'm living on salads.'

'Do you need to diet?' His appraising gaze swept over her neat figure. 'I would have said you were already too thin——Oh, excuse me, someone I know.' He ambled off, leaving a startled Linda to follow him with her eyes.

The nurse he was smiling down at was as short as Linda herself, but had stunning red hair, and she began to feel a surprising surge of jealousy. It was alarming as well as surprising, and she didn't know what to do about it. True, she would have liked hair as glorious as that of the nurse, but that wasn't why she was jealous!

She was still puzzling over the strange feeling when Jamie came strolling back, then drank his tea standing up, his eyes never leaving her face. 'I'll just take our cups back, then we'll be on our way—I'll see you in the visitors' car park,' he added, and, dismissed, Linda made her disconsolate way out of the hospital building, wishing Jamie smiled at her the way he had smiled at that pretty nurse.

He joined her after a few moments, looking tanned and healthy in his short-sleeved shirt and light cords. He was an immensely attractive man, and now that he'd shed the consultant demeanour, an immensely sexy one too, and Linda bent her head to unlock her car door. His hand on her arm prevented her, his fingers burning her. She almost snatched her arm away, and a strange expression crossed his face.

'I don't bite, Sister. You can leave your car here for a while, we'll go in mine,' he offered, but, stubbornly, she shook her head.

'No, I'd rather not. The car park gets pretty full, and I don't want Esmeralda standing out here in the sun all day,' she hurried on.

Jamie glanced at the Mini. 'Esmeralda, eh? Funny, my first motorbike was called that—I can't think why! Anyway, leave her here for now—we won't be long. Come on,' he ordered, leaving Linda no option but to get into his roomy car, wondering where they were going but deciding not to ask.

Instead of taking the road to the Clinic, Jamie turned off at the small crossroads, heading across country. It seemed at first that they were going to her cottage, but just before they reached the level crossing, he took a right turn along a tree-lined avenue, and stopped his car about halfway along.

The patient certainly lived in imposing surroundings, and it was the sort of house Linda would have liked herslf, detached and with a bit of breathing space, yet not isolated. It was set well back from the road, with a huge front garden full of colourful shrubs, including a magnificent magnolia, and she paused to admire it as she waited for Jamie to explain the reason for their visit.

When he didn't speak, she said lightly, 'You didn't tell me we were doing a domiciliary visit, Doctor.'

'We aren't, we're playing truant. This is where I live.' Jamie indicated the big house, and Linda's eyes widened.

'You certainly live in some style! I love that magnolia.' Now that she knew it was his home, she took more interest in the house itself. It was Georgian in style, partly creeper-covered, and probably had about four bedrooms, she judged. Too big for a lone divorced man—but perhaps Wanda shared it with him?

She wondered whether there might be a housekeeper, but Jamie produced a bunch of keys and let them into the house. The coolness of the tiled hall was a contrast to the heat outside, and Linda shivered a little.

'You might find it rather cold after being in the sun, Linda. Why don't you go right through to the sun lounge?' Jamie suggested, and Linda needed no second bidding. The sun lounge ran the whole length of the house and was unbearably hot. Then Jamie, coming unnoticed from the hall, put his hands on her shoulders and she immediately felt hotter than ever! But she didn't flinch, didn't try to get away. After all, it was meant as merely a friendly gesture, perhaps a gesture of reconciliation, a way of apologising for his treatment of her. She rather wished he'd found some other way to apologise, though! 'Too hot now, I suppose?' he said gently, and, dumbly, she nodded. 'Never mind, there's nothing like a laze by the pool. This way.'

She followed him out into a terrace which was shaded from the sun, and there, a few yards away, was the swimming pool she'd heard about from Nurse Craig. It gleamed, blue and inviting, and she could almost feel the refreshing water closing over her. What wouldn't she give for a dip right now!

'I wish I could offer you a bathe, but I don't think Wanda's swimsuit would fit you,' Jamie said lightly, and she smiled brightly, trying to disguise the pain his words had caused. Wanda *did* live with him, then. Well, it was only to be expected. Just because he was a psychiatrist, a father figure to many of his patients, it didn't mean that he wasn't a man first, with a healthy male's appetites.

'Wanda doesn't seem to be in. I'll have a look upstairs, she may be lying down,' Jamie went on. 'Make yourself at home.'

Yes, by all means have a look upstairs, Linda thought disconsolately. Don't hurry on *my* account. Unaccountably miserable, she wandered down the terrace steps towards the pool. Beside the pool there was a deck chair and a couple of sun-loungers. On top of one was a pair of sunglasses and a big, shady hat in bright pink. Linda stared at them for a moment, trying to visualise their owner. She would be tall, she decided, and slender. That she would be beautiful was a foregone conclusion. Nearly thirty, perhaps, a cultured and rich divorcee, someone glamorous, a fitting foil to the sort of friends Jamie obviously had, Linda's mind went on gloomily, remembering the woman they'd met in the restaurant. Yes, glamorous and shallow. She——

'Wanda was lying down, but she'll be here directly.' A smiling Jamie came running lightly down the steps. So at last she was to meet Wanda! Well, it would be interesting to see whether the picture she had built up was anyway near correct. That was the only advantage of meeting the woman, Linda decided, turning her gaze once more towards the pool.

'You look pensive, Linda. Has something upset you?' Jamie's smile was quizzical, and Linda forced herself to meet it bravely.

'I was just thinking how cruel it was of you to show me your swimming pool, knowing I hadn't a costume!' she said with an attempt at a laugh, but it didn't quite come off, and those pale eyes narrowed.

No, you *won't* read my mind! she thought crossly, but was saved from any comment Jamie might make when a husky voice hailed them from the top of the terrace.

Linda turned towards the sound, preparing herself for her first sight of the glamorous, trendy Wanda, but was completely taken aback when a woman began slowly to descend the steps. Jamie went forward to meet her, leaving Linda to pull herself together. Wanda's hair was certainly blonde, with streaks of grey showing through, and she must be well into her fifties!

'I'd like you to meet Linda, dear—Sister Linda Scott, my day patient sister. Linda, this is Wanda Hemsley. I've mentioned her before, I imagine.' Was there a hint of defensiveness in Jamie's voice?

Believing she had imagined it, Linda held out her hand, and Wanda beamed at her. 'Jamie keeps on about his day patient sister, and I begged him to bring you home! He has, at last!' Wanda laughed, her blue eyes crinkling.

Linda managed a polite 'How do you do, Mrs Hemsley?' but her surprise must have shown in her face, for Jamie smiled ruefully.

'I think Linda expected a youthful little redhead,' he said slowly, his eyes on Linda, who flushed guiltily, causing his smile to deepen.

'Well, I'm not youthful, a redhead *or* little!' Wanda chuckled. 'Do come and sit by the pool, Sister, and call me Wanda—everyone does! I'm afraid my swimsuits wouldn't fit you, though you could try one if you liked?' she offered, but Linda was quick to refuse. No way was she going into the house and up to the bedroom Wanda shared with Jamie! That was too much to ask of her.

'It's all right, really. I'd be glad to sit in the shade for a while. I burn easily and——'

'Of course, perfectly natural, you being a blonde. Such lovely hair! Hasn't Sister got lovely hair, Jamie?'

Wanda turned to Jamie with a smile, and he nodded appreciatively.

'Blondes are my favourite!' Tenderly he ruffled Wanda's abundant curls, and they smiled into each other's eyes, leaving Linda feeling very much the interloper. The sooner she got out of here, the better. They clearly loved each other, and if they weren't married there must be a good reason for it. Certainly she and Jamie were meant for each other, despite the obvious differences in their ages, and Linda tried to be glad for them both. She took up Wanda's invitation to sit in the shade and talk, and Jamie disappeared into the house, promising to return with a cool drink shortly.

'Isn't he a pet!' Wanda slipped off the caftan she had been wearing, displaying a generous-sized body clad in a black swimsuit. Perching the sunglasses on her nose and the pink hat on her head, she beamed at Linda. 'Tell me about yourself, Sister. Jamie says——'

'Oh, please call me Linda! Sister sounds so formal!' Linda managed a laugh, for, despite her crushed feelings, she was beginning to like the woman, though she wondered what they would find to talk about while Jamie was fetching the drinks. She doubted that they would have much in common.

She needn't have worried, for she didn't need to talk, Wanda did it all. In fact, once she was started it was impossible to stop her. After a few minutes, Linda began to see that Wanda was in as much need of tender loving care as any of their patients. The words poured forth like a fast-running stream, and Linda found that it wasn't necessary to do more than nod encouragingly, or smile every now and again—Wanda did the rest. She spoke of her early life as an aspiring actress, followed by an unhappy marriage. Then she smiled sadly.

'The only good thing about that marriage was my daughter Chrissie. She was a lovely girl—at least, I always thought so, but——' Wanda shrugged, and Linda wondered what was coming next. Then Jamie reappeared, bearing a tray of squash and biscuits, and the moment was lost.

Jamie settled himself beside Wanda after serving out the drinks, and Linda idly sipped her squash, wondering about the daughter. Apparently she had come to a bad end, and she wondered whether there was any connection with Jamie. Had he known Chrissie? Clearly Wanda bottled up her emotions far too much and needed a friendly ear to pour her troubles into.

'I was telling Linda about my Chrissie,' Wanda said suddenly, and Jamie started, nearly spilling his drink. Linda watched as a little dripped on to his shirt.

He dabbed at it irritably, without looking their way. 'What were you telling Linda about her?' he asked gently.

Wanda made a moue. 'Well, nothing, actually. I——'

'Perhaps that's just as well, Wanda dear. Anyway, Sister and I will have to go in a minute or two. We can't play truant *all* morning,' he reproved her.

'No, Jamie,' Wanda said meekly, then took off her sunglasses and gave Linda such an outrageous wink that she spluttered.

'Stop poking fun at me,' Jamie said mildly. 'Sister knows I have to be obeyed without question at all times! Isn't that right, Sister Scott?'

'Yes, sir, absolutely right,' Linda affirmed, causing Wanda to go off in paroxysms of laughter.

Abruptly he put his glass down, his eyes meeting Linda's. The signals were unmistakable—keep out of my private life, Sister. Well, she intended doing that, anyway. He was the one who had invited her here! Indignantly she got up, then indicated the tray. 'Would you like me to wash the glasses, Wanda? It won't take a minute.'

'No, no, dear! Leave it to me. It will give me something to occupy myself with while Jamie's at work.' Wanda, too, rose, her eyes kind as they rested on Linda. Then her gaze swept over Jamie, and there seemed to be some silent message going from one to the other. Linda had no idea what it was, but Wanda nodded as if satisfied, while Jamie looked decidedly discomfited.

'Take Sister—I mean Linda—back to work, then, Jamie. Shall you be late home?' Wanda enquired, and he shrugged, then grinned lazily, whatever had caused his discomfiture apparently forgotten.

'No, I won't be late.' He pecked Wanda on the cheek, then picked up the tray. 'I'll carry this in for you, then we must be away.'

'Jamie doesn't want me to talk about Chrissie, but I need to, Sister!' Wanda put a detaining hand on Linda's arm. 'I *have* to talk about her. She died, but we might have saved her! Jamie and I between us, we let her die!' There was a break in her voice, and swiftly Linda took both her hands in her own.

'I'm sure if there'd been a chance of saving Chrissie, Dr Grainger would have been able to,' Linda assured her, assuming that the daughter had committed suicide and that Jamie's skills hadn't been of use.

'Yes, I expect you're right, but we both loved her so. You couldn't *not* love Chrissie. Jamie tells me your young man's exactly the same,' Wanda went on surprisingly, and Linda opened her mouth to protest, when Jamie hailed her from the top of the terrace steps and she had no option but to go. Wanda hung on to her hand for a moment, though, and extracted a promise that Linda would call on her again. 'I'm always here, Linda. Do come and talk to me!' she urged.

'Of course I will—provided Dr Grainger agrees,' Linda said with a smile, then ran up the steps to where Jamie was waiting. 'Sorry! I couldn't get—I mean I——' she floundered.

'You were right the first time—you couldn't get away. Wanda's like that.' They both turned to wave to Wanda, who waved back energetically before resuming her seat on the sun-lounger, and tipping the bright hat over her eyes.

'She's a lonely woman,' Linda said as they reached Jamie's car.

'Very perceptive of you,' he commented. 'Yes, she needs to talk, and I thought a mental nurse was the right person for her to talk to. You're the only one in the Clinic I can trust not to upset her,' he went on, and Linda thanked him quietly.

She was here only because she was a trained mental nurse, and he thought Wanda needed someone like that to talk to. Naturally, she was flattered that he had chosen her, but it would have been nice to have been invited for her own sake!

'What happened about Mrs Skilton? Do you think she would have come?' she asked, anxious to change the subject.

'Mm? No, I don't suppose so, but I was in such a state I nearly subjected her to the flooding technique!' Jamie smiled grimly. 'There she stood, clutching one of those over-fed cats, and I marched her to the car, cat and all, before she had time to feel afraid! I've always believed desensitisation is a better treatment than throwing the sufferer in at the deep end, but——' He smiled ruefully at her.

'It's certainly *kinder* than flooding,' Linda agreed gently. 'Why were you in a state?' That Jamie would lose his temper with a patient was inconceivable. Surely it wasn't her absence that had thrown the unflappable psychiatrist?

He seemed about to explain, then apparently thought better of it. 'It was one of those mornings,' he said briefly, leaving Linda to make what she would of it.

'What happened then? Did she run back into the house?'

'No, she froze and couldn't—or wouldn't—move in either direction. Then the cat tried to wriggle free and I managed to get them both back to the house. I was afraid I'd have a screaming woman on my hands, but I think fright had rendered her incapable of speech!'

'I wonder if we *can* get her to the Clinic,' Linda mused. 'Perhaps with the cat. I told her the patients might like to see one of them.'

'I know. She told me Sister Scott wanted animals at the Clinic!' Jamie smiled, his annoyance apparently forgotten, and Linda felt the sun was shining again.

She hated to breach the fragile peace, but went on slowly, 'About Wanda—she's asked me to go back to see her and I said I would if I had your permission. She wants to talk about Chrissie, but if you'd rather I didn't. . .'

'She needs to talk about her, and we do, often. I suppose I'm the one who finds it painful to dredge up old miseries, not Wanda.' Jamie stopped the car in a layby, and turned to her with a faint smile hovering about his mouth.

'Wanda seems to think you might have saved Chrissie.

Was she suicidal? I——' She stopped, alarmed at the expression on his face.

Varied emotions chased themselves across his usually expressionless face, and he glanced at her sharply. 'No, she wasn't suicidal—far from it. Chrissie loved life, and life loved Chrissie. Her death was an accident, but Wanda can't see it that way. She's convinced that one or both of us could have saved her. But she was impetuous, Linda, a born adventurer. She would have died young, anyway. Neither of us could go on shielding her from the results of her own folly.'

He lapsed into silence, staring straight ahead, but Linda knew he wasn't seeing the long, winding road, he was looking back into the past, a past that contained an elusive girl called Chrissie—obviously someone he had tried desperately to save. Jamie's fingers tightened on the wheel, and she longed to reach out and cover them with her own hands, letting the warmth of her own personality chase away the ghosts that plagued him. But she had no right! No right at all.

Instead, she made a small, sympathetic gesture, and Jamie smiled down at her. 'You're easy to talk to, Linda. That's what I like about you,' he confided, and she tried to look pleased, though it seemed a somewhat tame compliment. 'Of course, what I mean is, you're easy to talk to when we're not pulling in opposite directions!' he added, and she waved her fist at him.

'We aren't *always* pulling in opposite directions! I think we. . .' Her voice trailed off as she read the expression in Jamie's eyes. Whatever the consultant psychiatrist saw in her, right at that moment it wasn't the fact that she was easy to talk to.

Silently he set the car in motion again. Shaken by that one moment of drama, Linda sat back and closed her eyes. She had the beginnings of a headache, she had never felt less like work, and there was still the problem of Paul's whereabouts, not to mention her need for Jamie. If the patients had problems, they weren't the only ones—she had accumulated a few herself!

CHAPTER FIVE

'MRS ELLERSHAW? I'm Linda Scott, the day patient sister.' Linda smiled a welcome to the tall, very thin lady who had arrived for an in-depth interview with Jamie Grainger.

The smile was returned nervously, and Betty Ellershaw shook Linda's hand. Her palms were damp with perspiration, and Linda sought for some way to put the woman at her ease. 'Won't you come in and sit down? I'll ask for some tea, shall I?' she offered, as the patient preceded her into the interview-room.

'Oh! It isn't what I expected,' Mrs Ellershaw exclaimed, waving a hand to indicate the homeliness of the surroundings. Linda had made a few changes to the interview-room, having found it a little too clinical when she had first arrived. Now, bright chintzy curtains flapped gently in the breeze from the open window, matching the covers on the comfortable settee and armchairs. There were plenty of chairs scattered about the room, and Linda indicated that the patient might sit where she chose.

'It's only in cartoons that people visiting a psychiatrist lie back on a big black couch!' she laughed. 'Dr Grainger will probably sit on the settee, or over by the window—he's a fresh air fiend, by the way!' she added, liking to add a few bits of personal information, just to make the patients feel at ease. 'I like fresh air, but a little goes a long way,' she added, and Mrs Ellershaw nodded vigorously.

'My husband—my late husband—he always slept with the bedroom window open, even in the winter. Such a dreadful habit!' She shuddered. 'You can imagine what it was like when the snow was on the ground! I always had the side nearest the window, as well. But it was no use moaning, he would have his own way. Now I'm glad I let him, because he's gone and I'm still here,' she went on, half to herself, and Linda was careful not to interrupt her. Whatever the patient said of relevance would be noted in her personal file and might prove useful during the course of her treatment. What she told Linda or the other nurses she might not think to tell the psychiatrist. Indeed, it was often the case, as in general hospitals, that the patients would tell nurses things they wouldn't dream of mentioning to doctors, either through embarrassment or because they didn't think the information relevant, or, more often, because they didn't like to bother the doctor.

'It seems so unfair that he's gone and I'm still here!' Mrs Ellershaw burst out suddenly, just as Jamie himself appeared in the doorway. He smiled at her, holding out his hands in a welcoming way, and Mrs Ellershaw clutched his hand like a drowning man clutching at a straw.

Linda tried to make herself as unobtrusive as possible, not wanting to destroy the rapport that seemed to have sprung up instantly between patient and doctor. It didn't often happen, sometimes it took weeks, even months, before doctor and patient were at ease and fully trusted each other, but clearly Jamie was just what Mrs Ellershaw had been waiting for, and Linda tried to edge out of the room.

'Don't go, Sister,' Jamie ordered, and Linda stopped.

'Shall I get some tea, Doctor?' she queried. 'Mrs Ellershaw would like a cup, I know.'

'Yes, if you would. Get one of the students to make it, then come back, please,' he said, and Linda did as she was bid. She was waylaid by another patient on her way back, then the new staff nurse asked her advice, so she kept patient and psychiatrist waiting longer than expected, and Jamie's glance was cool as she tapped on the door, then entered quietly.

'Ah, here's Sister Scott at last,' he said softly, and Linda smiled at them both. Only her eyes challenged the psychiatrist, and Mrs Ellershaw couldn't have been aware of that.

The woman turned to her, clearly delighted that she was to have company. 'I've been telling Doctor—about my husband sleeping with the window open, dear,' she began, then talked solidly for the next twenty minutes or so. She had the need to talk, and no one else to talk to, and Linda didn't interrupt her. Nor did Jamie, who relaxed on the big, comfortable settee and smiled and nodded at the patient from time to time.

Linda doubted if Mrs Ellershaw saw his encouraging gestures, she was too wrapped up in her own problems and her own guilt. For some reason, she blamed herself for her much older husband's perfectly natural death, and Linda was reminded of poor Wanda, who blamed herself for her daughter's death. In both cases, it was no one's fault, and she wondered how Jamie would approach Mrs Ellershaw's insistence that, in some way, she could have saved her husband.

Rather to her surprise, Jamie didn't refer to the man, even when Mrs Ellershaw made one or two pointed references to him and his death. He changed the subject and went on to ask the usual questions that were asked at these interviews—what sort of childhood she'd had, how many there were in the family, any early memories that had stayed in her mind, and so on.

It was clear that she enjoyed talking about herself, but enjoyed talking about the past even more, and she had a rich fund of reminiscences about wartime, the queues, ration books, the day a bomb dropped nearby, and Linda asked her several questions about the war, once the flow of monologue seemed to be drying up. By the time the interview was over, it was past lunchtime, and Jamie suggested that they might all lunch together in the canteen, to Mrs Ellershaw's evident delight.

After lunch, Linda gave her a lift home, then arrived back at the Clinic to find that her relaxation classes hadn't taken place. Normally she took charge of the class once a week and attended them whenever her other duties permitted, but Mrs Ellershaw had taken up most of her day and she had supposed that the new staff nurse, Anne Redmond, would take over.

'I'd no idea you wanted me to do the relaxations, Sister!' Nurse Redmond was almost wringing her hands in dismay, and Linda hastened to reassure her.

'It doesn't matter now, really. But we always have relaxation classes just before the ladies go home. It might seem like an odd time to have them, but they appreciate it—it recharges their batteries before they have to face the cruel world again, or so they tell me. Whenever I'm away, Nurse Craig or yourself will have to do them— where is she, anyway?' It was unusual for Muriel Craig not to be bustling about, and she was a far better organiser than Nurse Redmond was shaping up to be.

'Oh, there was some guy hanging around. Used to be a patient here, I think. Muriel took him by the hand and marched him away! They're still in the visitors' room,' the nurse went on. 'It's all right—I *did* look in on them a while back, but she didn't want any help,' she went on as Linda opened her mouth to ask just that question.

'I'd better have a word with her, then. Ask the ladies if they still want their relaxation, will you?'

Wondering who the ex-patient was, and why he had come to day patients, Linda knocked quietly on the door of the visitors' room and was relieved when Nurse Craig came to the door, inching it open.

'Oh, it's you again, Staff Nurse!' Nurse Craig said brightly, and Linda's eyes widened. 'There's no sign of Sister yet, I suppose? Well, Mr Winterton will have to see her another time. I knew she'd be busy,' the nurse hurried on, then closed the door firmly, after giving Linda a warning look.

Silently Linda walked away, sending up a prayer of thankfulness for Muriel Craig. Paul had come looking for her, demanding yet more of her time, despite her warning that he wasn't welcome during working hours. Nurse Craig mustn't be left to carry the burden alone, though, and Linda took a couple of turns around the clinic then walked briskly back. This time she didn't wait for her knock to be answered. When she opened the door, it was indeed Paul there—he was reading to Nurse Craig from his manuscript, and Linda raised a brow.

'Hello, Paul. Staff Nurse said you wanted to see me.' She smiled her thanks at Muriel, who gave a weary sigh. 'Paul's just going now, Nurse—if you wouldn't mind doing the relaxations? They appear to have been overlooked today,' Linda went on pleasantly, and Nurse Craig made her escape, no doubt thankfully.

'You shouldn't have sent her away, Lindy,' Paul protested, waving his manuscript. 'She was enjoying the chapter—it's the part where the detective confronts the murderer, or so he thinks. Only it isn't the murderer.'

'Ah, yes, that part. You had me fooled there,' Linda admitted, aware that Paul had written a good whodunnit. 'Anyway, Nurse has work to do and you're holding up the routine. Will you be in for supper?' She stood by the door, holding it open, and Paul took the hint.

'I can see I'm not wanted,' he said cheerfully enough, and Linda smiled at him.

'Not during working hours, but you know that already,' she pointed out, her smile taking the sting out of her words. 'If my boss should catch you, I'll be the one who gets into trouble!'

'I doubt that—I think he likes you. Who wouldn't?' Paul teased, then dropped a kiss on her cheek before hurrying out, whistling a merry tune. Linda put a hand to her cheek, half amused and half angry at his gesture. Despite that awful weekend with his sister, he simply wouldn't learn! Yet he had his disarming ways and could be very charming indeed when he wanted to be. Paul had a lot going for him, and if the book found a publisher, she might, at last, get rid of her unwelcome lodger!

'Busy, Sister?' A chilly voice froze Linda where she stood, and she dropped her hand, the smile fading from her mouth.

'I'm always busy, Doctor,' she answered calmly, wondering just how much Jamie had seen, and afraid he had seen all too much!

'I'm glad to hear that,' he said mildly enough, but there was an ominous gleam in his eyes. 'I can always find you extra work if we're under-using you,' he carried on, and Linda began audibly counting to ten.

'Ten!' she finished triumphantly, then marched back

to her office, head held high. She thought she had
handled him rather well, and was a bit put out when he
followed her. The fragile peace seemed as though it was
to be broken again!

'I should try counting to twenty, Sister—ten isn't
enough in this place!' Jamie commented, as he wrapped
his long body around a chair. 'I was about to ask you if
Winterton was back yet, but I see he is.'

Linda sighed. 'Yes, he's back! He turned up on
Sunday night and wouldn't say where he'd been. It
looked as though he'd been sleeping rough, and we had
a bit of a row when I wouldn't let him into the sitting-
room until he'd had a bath,' she went on crossly, and
Jamie chuckled.

'I can just see you wielding the big stick, Linda—all
five foot one of you!'

'There's no need to mock me just because I'm little!
Anyway, when I'm angry, I forget how little I am,' she
confessed, with a laugh. 'I told him he might have picked
up a flea, and he was most indignant. It's no disgrace—
the disgrace lies in keeping them, and I'm afraid I rather
lectured poor Paul!'

'You're wasting your time, Linda. The poor Pauls of
this world don't listen,' Jamie commented bitterly, and
she wondered if he was thinking of Chrissie.

'What about Wanda? Is it all right if I visit her some
time—or would you rather I didn't?' Linda put in, one
thought leading easily into the next, though it must have
seemed a puzzling change of subject to Jamie.

'Wanda? Yes, I suppose you could.' He didn't sound
very enthusiastic, and Linda didn't like to labour the
point.

'You'd rather I didn't.' It was a statement rather than
a question, and Jamie eyed her sharply.

'Did I say that?'

'Well, no, but it's pretty obvious you think Wanda and I would be chewing over your private life and——'

'Rubbish! There isn't anything to "chew over", as you put it!' Jamie almost snarled, and Linda gazed at him in astonishment. They had been getting along so well, but somehow she must have touched a raw nerve and set their relationship right back to square one. Before she could think of a suitably cutting remark, Jamie's stern features relaxed into a smile. 'I'm sorry, Sister Scott.'

'That's perfectly all right, Dr Grainger,' she said formally, and Jamie's lips twitched.

'Anyway, Wanda's throwing a party on Friday—or so she informed me this morning. Do you want to come?'

Linda hesitated. A party at Wanda's was the last thing she wanted. Jamie waited patiently for her answer, and she got the feeling that he actually wanted her to come. 'I—may I bring Paul? He loves parties,' she said flatly, and he seemed about to refuse, then shrugged.

'If you wish. I can't pretend he'll be welcome, but Wanda will take him in hand, no doubt. It's only a small party. Perhaps we might have a barbecue, if it's fine, or just a buffet. Jenny Meacham's coming—you remember? We met her in Brighton.'

Oh, yes, she rememberd Jenny Meacham very well, and the idea of the party looked even less enticing, but Linda refused to back out. 'I'll look forward to Friday, then. Thank you,' she said softly.

'Are we friends again, then?' he asked. 'I wonder for how long?'

'That rather depends on you,' Linda pointed out. 'You're the one with the short fuse! I never know where I am,' she complained, and it was Jamie's turn to look astonished.

'A short fuse? Have I?'

'Yes! You're always finding fault with me, blowing me up just when I think we're getting on well. Surely you're aware of it?' He really was surprised. Could it be that he didn't know the effect he had on her? Well, no, he couldn't possibly know the *main* effect he had on her, but that was another story!

'That must have been what Wanda meant. She said there was a chemistry between us—she told me she could almost see the sparks,' he went on thoughtfully.

'That's electricity, not chemistry. Anyway,' Linda rushed on, 'I must away. I have a hungry lodger to feed.' Deliberately, she introduced Paul into the conversation, not wanting him to realise just how perceptive Wanda had been!

'Is there electricity between you and Winterton, I wonder?' Jamie mused, then went on before Linda could think of a suitable remark, 'Do you suppose we might cause an electrical storm if we happened to kiss again? That's an interesting theory, Sister Scott—we must put it to the test some time. Now,' he went on calmly, 'how did you find Mrs Ellershaw this morning?'

Glad of the change of subject, Linda pondered her answer for a moment. Even though they had left personal matters, that little spark of chemistry, electricity or whatever, was still between them, making concentrating on work rather difficult for her. Of course, it made no difference to Jamie. *He* was used to women worshipping the ground he walked on—well, *she* wasn't about to worship him, that was for certain! 'I think, basically, that she's lonely. She feels guilty, certainly, though without any reason as far as I can see,' she said at last. 'I wouldn't call her mentally ill, though. She simply needs the chance to grieve properly, get it out of her system. She——'

'Good!' Jamie broke in. 'That's exactly my feeling, Sister,' he went on formally, and Linda saw Staff Nurse Redmond hovering in the doorway.

Although the nurse spoke to Linda, her eyes kept straying to the doctor. 'I wondered whether you needed any help with anything, Sister? Nurse Craig's doing the relaxations, and there doesn't seem to be anything else.'

It was Jamie who answered, with his easy smile. 'Then I suggest you join the relaxation classes, Staff. You'll have to cope with it sooner or later—might as well have twenty minutes' rest while you can.'

Linda watched the effect Jamie's smile had on the nurse. Clearly, if Dr Grainger had told Nurse Redmond to jump in the sea, she would have done so!

When the nurse had gone, Linda said lightly, 'Another conquest for the handsome doctor!'

Jamie didn't share her amusement. 'I do not seek conquests, Sister Scott! If my pleasant manner causes women to throw themselves at my feet, that's entirely up to them! I certainly don't go out of my way to charm them,' he added.

'No, you don't,' Linda agreed quietly. 'But charm them you do, nevertheless. It's only me who gets the sharp edge of your tongue,' she said, trying to keep the resentment out of her voice. Here wasn't the place to air personal grievances, but whatever charm he turned on, very little of it ever came her way—unless he wanted her help!

'Do I keep the sharp edge of my tongue for you?' Jamie sounded amused. 'I wasn't aware I *had* a sharp edge! Anyway, we're supposed to be discussing a patient. Though. . .'

He paused, and Linda prompted, 'Yes, Doctor?'

'Though when you're sitting there looking so pretty, it's hard sometimes to concentrate on psychiatry,' he murmured. 'What about Mrs Ellershaw, then? What treatment would you advise?'

Startled, Linda couldn't think straight for a moment. He'd said she was pretty! Actually paid *her* a compliment! 'I—you mentioned ECT to her, but I don't think so—not in her case,' she managed, and Jamie nodded his approval.

'No, I feel what she terms "the shock treatment" is inappropriate for her. Perhaps anti-depressants later. But for now, plenty of TLC and company, a chance to talk. You can get the CPN involved,' he added, then went on to discuss all the patients attending that day, while Linda made notes.

This was what she liked best—these times when Jamie forgot to provoke her, didn't mention Paul Winterton, just concentrated on patients and their treatment, asking her opinion about each one. At least that was one point in Jamie's favour: he wasn't one of those consultants who considered that nurses were there only to do the doctor's bidding. He expected, even demanded, her opinions, her thoughts on treatment, making her feel she was an important member of the therapeutic team. Because of that, she felt she could put up with his occasional jibes about poor Paul, his short fuse where she was concerned, his occasional fault-finding.

'Do you approve of me, Sister?' Jamie's calm voice broke into her thoughts, and she flushed, aware now that she must have been staring at him while she mentally assessed his good points!

'Well—possibly. Occasionally. Now and then,' she went on, and he chuckled, his eyes laughing at her.

Linda had the absurd feeling that she wanted to drown in those light eyes. They were the colour of the winter sea and seemed to be drawing her in, a dangerous undercurrent whirling about her, slowly dragging her beneath the waves. . . With a surprise effort, she pulled herself together, aware that this man was just as dangerous as a strong current in the sea. He could drag her under, drown her in waves of pleasure, without even trying. But he wasn't for her—Wanda needed him. She was beginning to realise that she herself needed him far more than Wanda did. It was a disturbing thought, and, shaken, she began to ask about Gwen Skilton, but the words died unsaid as she became aware of Jamie's expression.

He seemed about to speak, and Linda prayed for the telephone to ring, someone to interrupt them, anything at all, just to break the spell he was casting over her— for it could end only in heartache. But instead of speaking, he glanced down at his hands, then picked up his notes and walked out without his customary smile and polite word of goodbye.

Unmoving, Linda watched him, feeling that her whole future had just walked out of the door.

CHAPTER SIX

THE moment she parked her car and switched off the engine, Linda could hear the noise from the party. Jamie had called it a small party, but it didn't sound small to her! Judging by the number of cars parked in his driveway, it was a big, crowded affair, and she was in two minds about going. With so many people milling around, surely Jamie wouldn't notice if she didn't turn up? And if he noticed, would he care, anyway?

It was but a small step from thought to deed, and Linda had her hand on the ignition key, ready to start the car again, when she realised how foolish and, yes, how cowardly she was being. The guests wouldn't eat her, for heaven's sake! She was suffering from a Jamie-phobia and was as much in need of advice as some of the patients! No matter how much it hurt her seeing Wanda and Jamie together, so obviously in love, she would grin and bear it, somehow. With such a big crowd, she could soon lose herself once she had thanked her host and hostess.

Half wishing that Paul had agreed to come with her, she ventured round the side of the house, where Jamie had told her the party was to be held, and the first face she spotted was that of her new staff nurse. Startled and a little put out that Jamie hadn't told her, Linda made her way towards Nurse Redmond, who was hanging on the arm of a tall man Linda didn't know.

'Oh, hello, Sister.' Anne Redmond was giggling away as she drank from a mug. 'Fancy seeing you here! I wasn't going to come, but the Chief insisted. This is my boyfriend, Peter—Dr Peter Sayers. He's starting at the Summerheath next week.' She indicated the tall young man, and Linda muttered a few polite words before escaping to find Jamie.

She ran him to ground beside the barbecue, the delicious smell drawing her to his side. He turned at her approach, and she suppressed a smile at seeing the debonair psychiatrist wrapped in an all-enveloping butcher's apron!

'Glad you could make it, Linda. Brought lover-boy, have you?' asked Jamie, his eyes and his attention on the task in hand, and a mutinous Linda glared at his back.

'If you mean Paul, no, he didn't want to leave his book. It's in a critical stage and he's trying to get it finished. He's working very hard,' she added tartly, and Jamie swung round, that lazy smile breaking out.

'I'm sure he is. Have you seen Wanda? She's been wondering where you were,' he added. 'Had second thoughts about coming?' he suggested.

'No! But Paul wanted me to stay in and do a bit of typing for him, and by the time I'd got him settled and cooked his supper, I left it rather late getting ready,' she confessed.

'I wouldn't have known you dressed in a hurry,' Jamie remarked. 'You look rather special in that swirly thing.'

'That swirly thing' was her newest acquisition, a multi-coloured full-length skirt that swirled about her as she walked. She had teamed it with a silk shirt and felt foolishly happy that Jamie approved of her ensemble. Her black strappy sandals had high heels, and for once she didn't feel at such a disadvantage when talking to him.

'See? I'm almost up to your shoulder now! I've grown since yesterday,' she joked, but Jamie wasn't smiling.

Instead, he gazed down at her. It was a brooding sort of look, and Linda swallowed nervously, preparing to take flight if he tried to touch her. They were in full view of everyone, so that wasn't likely, but the feeling persisted. 'You're special, Linda. I don't like to see you wasting your life on that scoundrel,' he said instead, and Linda felt as if he had slapped her face.

'Paul isn't a scoundrel, and who am I special to, if it isn't to him?' She almost shouted the words. Telling her she was special didn't mean what she so very much wanted it to mean!

'What will he do once he's finished this world-shattering best-seller?' Jamie went on, wiping his hands on a cloth. He beckoned to a guest and indicated the barbecue. 'Robert can see to this now. Come on, I'll introduce you around.' Taking her none too gently by the arm, he marched her away, steering her towards a small group surrounding Wanda. 'Well?' he demanded, when Linda remained silent.

'Well what? I shouldn't have thought Paul's future was any concern of yours, but I suppose he'll leave once I've ceased to be of use to him.' It was true, she felt. Paul was at last growing away from her, and she couldn't be more pleased, both for herself *and* for him. Once she had finished typing his book, he would drift away, perhaps returning from time to time—and probably not at all if he found someone else to latch on to, she reflected wryly.

'That's sad, Linda. I'm glad in a way, but it's always hurtful when a beautiful love dies,' Jamie said unexpectedly. They were on the edge of Wanda's entourage, and she hadn't noticed them yet. Linda could hear her laughter as someone cracked a joke.

'Wanda's in good form tonight. I'm glad for her, she needs company,' she murmured.

'We're talking about you and Paul Winterton—leave Wanda out of this!' Jamie snapped.

'Now just you look here, Dr Grainger,' Linda began, 'whatever happens between Paul and myself is no one's business but ours!'

'Isn't it? No, I suppose not.' Jamie sounded sad, and she glanced at him sharply, but his expression gave nothing away. 'If you love the guy, I'm sad that things haven't worked out for you, that's all.'

'But I don't love him! Haven't I been saying that ever since I started at the Clinic? He's just a lodger, and when he goes——'

'Are you trying to tell me that you share your home with a young, healthy male, yet don't share your bed?' Jamie's grip was beginning to hurt now, and Linda tried to pull away.

He let her go and she almost fell against him. By now they were beginning to attract attention, and she waved to Wanda, determined to break off this conversation before they came to blows!

'Linda, my dear! Welcome!' Wanda beckoned to her, and Linda thankfully left her boss where he was. He could go back to his barbecue for all she cared! He had no right to keep enquiring into her private life. He had certainly been tight-lipped enough about his *own* personal life!

Wanda introduced her to several of her friends, including the sharp-tongued Jenny Meacham, who eyed Linda in surprise.

'Fancy seeing you here, Miss Scott!' she exclaimed, her sharp gaze taking in every detail of Linda's ensemble.

'She isn't *Miss* Scott, she's *Sister* Scott,' Wanda declared with a warm smile. 'She's Jamie's day patient sister at the Clinic,' she went on, and Mrs Meacham's face cleared.

'So that's it! I thought it strange, Jamie wining and dining a lovely young female while Wanda languished at home! You're one of his *staff*!' she emphasised, but Linda made no comment. She wanted to, but luckily Jenny Meacham's attention was caught by another guest, and the moment passed.

'You mustn't mind Jenny,' Wanda whispered, as she took Linda by the arm and moved away from the admiring circle. 'She isn't very happy with Robert and she can't bear to see anyone else happy. That's life.' She gave a little sigh, and Linda realised the woman was thinking about Jamie—a Jamie who was himself now surrounded by friends, most of them female, Linda noted cynically. He seemed to have forgotten poor Wanda entirely, so they strolled together around the garden and down to the small orchard at the rear.

Wanda glanced up at the fruit trees. 'I think Jamie will have quite a good harvest this year. Better than last year, anyway.'

'Does he expect you to pick the apples? If he can't be bothered, I'd be happy to come and help you,' Linda offered.

'That's a wonderful idea! When they're ready, I'll ring Jamie and we'll both come and pick them for him!'

Puzzled, Linda said, 'But I thought you lived here? Are you going away, then?'

'Oh, no! This is Jamie's home. I thought you knew that?' Now it was Wanda's turn to look puzzled. 'I thought you knew about me and Jamie? Perhaps not,' she murmured, and Linda didn't wait to hear any more.

'I'd better get back and see if Jamie wants any help,' she said awkwardly. 'As I work for him, he might expect me to earn my meal!' she joked, and Wanda gave her a sharp look.

'I expect he'll be glad of your company anyway, my dear. He likes you.'

'I hope he likes *all* his staff, Wanda! It wouldn't do if he hated us, would it? Oh, by the way, I saw our new staff nurse earlier—are all the Clinic staff here? No one mentioned coming,' Linda went on, and Wanda shrugged.

'If you mean that tall girl, I don't think Jamie actually invited her, it was more a case of her inviting herself. Muriel Craig usually comes, but it's her anniversary at the weekend and her husband's taking her out to dinner, I believe.'

That was true, and explained Nurse Craig's absence. 'What about the others? I haven't seen anyone else,' Linda persisted, but Wanda didn't seem to know.

'Most of them are my friends, people from what Jamie calls "the fringe of show business", just minor actors, extras, that sort of person. I used to be on the stage,' she went on, with a deprecating gesture. 'It was years ago, of course, and I was never very good!' she went on honestly. 'I was so glad when Chrissie didn't get grease-paint in her blood, but——'

'Wanda, if ever you want to talk about Chrissie, I've Jamie's permission to come and see you. Get it out of your system,' Linda urged. 'The longer you keep it bottled up, the more poisonous it grows. Chrissie wouldn't want you to suffer, I'm sure.'

'I doubt that Chrissie would care either way,' was the

surprising answer. 'Chrissie was such a serene girl, with a lovely smile and such a beautiful face,' Wanda went on dreamily. 'Nothing bothered her, ever, nothing and no one. She never looked her age, either. Even when she got to thirty, she might easily have passed for a girl in her teens. Her face was completely unlined, her smile radiant. . .' She broke off, and Linda nodded understandingly.

What Wanda was describing was the face of someone with what psychiatrists called 'an hysterical personality'. Paul was that type of person. It was a personality defect rather than an actual mental illness, and as such, there was no cure. It wasn't actually psychopathy, though she knew Paul veered in that direction.

'I understand, Wanda. But please remember I'm here if ever you feel you have to talk.'

There was a shared moment of understanding, then Jamie hailed them from the foot of the terrace, and Linda whirled round, wondering how long he had been there. He strolled over to them, his usual pleasant smile no longer in evidence, and Linda bit her lip, wondering whether she was to be criticised for talking to Wanda. He seemed afraid she would learn too much about his personal life, but she never intended to pry. It was typical of the man that he should think the worst of her!

Wanda went to meet him, arms outstretched in welcome, and Linda watched them, her heart crying out within her, but it was a silent cry and no one would ever know just how much she was beginning to care for Jamie Grainger. She swallowed the lump that rose into her throat, but knew her eyes must be over-bright from the tears she was keeping back, and when Jamie and Wanda came over to her, she saw his eyes narrow. She felt vulnerable, naked, even, under his searching gaze, and she tried to keep her face as expressionless as Jamie's own. 'I ought to circulate, I suppose—is there anyone else here from the Clinic?' she asked Jamie.

'There shouldn't have been, though sometimes I invite Muriel, but Staff Nurse Redmond said how much she enjoyed barbecues, so I'm afraid I invited her,' he said wryly, then turned as several others joined them, including the nurse herself.

Linda noticed that Anne had left Dr Sayers now, and was smiling provocatively at Jamie. They were much of a height, and Linda felt excluded. Then Wanda touched her arm, and she followed her hostess to the barbecue area, where Robert Meacham was serving the food.

Robert, by contrast to his wife, was a pleasant, if slightly vague man, with a similar theatrical manner. 'He's an actor,' Wanda confided. 'Aren't you, darling? Quite my favourite actor.'

Robert beamed. 'Well, hardly, not these days. I'm permanently resting, I'm afraid. Taken an office job, bit of security,' he explained, handing Linda a plate of sausage and tomato. 'The chops aren't quite done, and there are baked potatoes over there—with plenty of butter and calorie-laden stuff to go on them!' he joked, and Linda wandered away with her plate, wondering whether she ought to rescue Jamie from the nurse.

Then she heard his distinctive laugh and, glancing around, saw him and Anne Redmond over by the terrace. He seemed to be enjoying himself, no matter that he had insisted he hadn't intended inviting the girl. If he wanted Anne's company, why couldn't he have said so, instead of being devious about it? Linda rejoined the group at the barbecue, determined to enjoy the evening, and put Jamie from her mind.

It was he who sought her out later on, and she was

glad to see that her staff nurse was nowhere in evidence. 'Enjoying yourself?' He indicated the frankfurter that Linda was halfway through, and she nodded, her mouth full. He chuckled, white teeth gleaming, his eyes half closed. Another sensuous look! she thought crossly.

'The chicken was delicious, absolutely out of this world!' she enthused, once she had finished her mouthful. She licked the last bit of butter from her lips, aware that Jamie's eyes were following the gesture.

'Would you like to see my exercise parlour?' he asked. 'It's tantamount to showing you my etchings, but I promise not to take advantage of you!' he added lightly, seeing her hesitation.

Not wanting to seem cowardly, Linda accepted the invitation, and they strolled companionably towards the house. 'It's around the back—you probably saw the building when you came to the pool. Wanda calls it my massage parlour but it's hardly that!'

'You haven't got a glamorous Swedish masseuse to soothe you after a hard day's work, then?'

'Unfortunately no, but it isn't because I haven't had offers!' Jamie said lightly, then stood aside for her to enter the low stone building. She had seen it before, but had assumed it was a storehouse, or changing-rooms.

'You could set up your own business here!' she commented, taking in the exercise bikes, two of them, she noticed in passing. Then there were weights stacked neatly in a corner, several exercise machines of the push-and-pull variety, plus a sauna bath.

'There are skipping ropes, sandbags to make exercising harder, that sort of thing—in that cupboard over there.' He turned to smile at her, and without thinking, she took a step back. 'Should you want to use them at any time, just let me know,' he said quietly, apparently not noticing her movement.

That would be fine for later, when Jamie wasn't with her, but right now all she wanted was to get away. The building was small and she felt locked in, imprisoned, with Jamie only inches away. She knew he was about to kiss her even before he did so. Knew also that she ought to turn and run, resist him when she felt his hands rest lightly on her shoulders, but she didn't. Nor did she resist when he tilted back her chin, forcing her to meet his gaze.

'Linda, oh, Linda.' His voice was soft, a mere caress, and never had her name sounded so wonderful. She heard sweet music coming from a thousand heavenly choirs, and would have been prepared to swear that the stars descended from the heavens and whirled about her as their lips met, gently at first, then with a searing intensity that took her breath away.

'No, please,' she breathed, when his mouth left hers long enough for her to speak. 'You mustn't. I——' Then his questing mouth found hers again, and there was no more need of words.

'Linda,' he murmured, as his lips left hers and trailed a soft, sweet path down her cheek, to her throat, then the lobes of her ears.

She shivered as his tongue gently probed her ear, then he kissed the corner of her mouth and she almost died with the ecstasy of it all. Nothing had prepared her for Jamie Grainger, dark passion blended with a degree of tenderness she found almost irresistible.

Almost, but not quite. The pain in her heart was unbearable as she thought of poor Wanda, and she tried unsuccessfully to prise herself from his arms. Jamie merely tightened his embrace, gazing down at her with such a look of love that for a moment she nearly believed he *did* love her. Remember Wanda, she told herself, renewing her efforts to free herself. 'Please let me go, Jamie—someone might come in!' she said urgently. 'Nurse Redmond might see us,' she added, and that did the trick.

With a sigh, he released her, still holding her by one hand, unwilling to let her go completely. 'Yes, we don't want Nurse Redmond gossiping about us, do we?' he agreed, with a faint smile.

'No, we certainly don't!' Linda said fervently, wondering whether he might be kissing Anne Redmond like that later on tonight. Who could say? He was such an enigma that anything was possible. And he was the one who had told her kissing Paul in public was unprofessional and totally unacceptable for a sister at the Summerheath Clinic!

Resentment flared for an instant, and Linda turned on him. 'You've no right to lecture *me* on how a sister at the clinic ought to behave! What about you? Who gave you the right to kiss me, trifle with my feelings? I suppose you think I haven't *got* any feelings!' she almost howled. 'In future, I suggest you save your kisses for your ladyfriends!'

Jamie's eyes mocked her. 'You're absolutely right, Sister Scott. I promise to do that in future,' he said agreeably, and with a choked-off sob, Linda fled, almost tripping over the exercise bike in her urgent need to escape. He was cruel, cruel! He was simply toying with her, perhaps to make Wanda jealous. Whatever the reason, she wanted nothing further to do with him. Poor Wanda was welcome to him, but Linda couldn't help feeling the woman deserved better than the philandering Jamie Grainger!

CHAPTER SEVEN

'I HAVE to keep touching things, Doctor, and always an even number of times.' The patient's confession was obviously painful to her, and Linda leaned forward and smiled encouragingly. She was rewarded by a touchingly grateful look as the patient, Miss Brent, continued, 'Usually it's ten times, but sometimes six or eight will do. Then I have to count things—the pattern on the curtains, cracks between the paving stones, that sort of thing. Then I have to start all over again in case I've missed any the first time,' she went on, staring straight ahead, the group in the room apparently forgotten.

This was one of the ward rounds where Jamie had allowed the students to be present. There were usually one or two students, general as well as psychiatric, and this time they were all general nursing students. They were crowded into the interview-room, together with the ward doctor, a social worker and the psychologist, plus Linda and Jamie himself. She had often thought it must be an ordeal for patients to explain their actions, discuss their most intimate thoughts in front of an audience of a dozen or so people, but Miss Brent didn't seem to mind. Nor did most of the others, she had to admit. They seemed to have the urge to unburden themselves in front of as many people as possible—something Linda herself would have hated. Yet for some, it was therapeutic, and certainly several minds getting to grips with one patient's problem was immensely helpful.

Once or twice Jamie, soft-voiced, asked Miss Brent a

question, but no one else spoke. There were several questions Linda was bursting to ask, but she knew the answers would be forthcoming in due course, and it was up to Jamie to control the interview. It was a learning session for the students too, and Linda had plans to involve them in every aspect of the Clinic's work.

She cast a sidelong glance at Jamie, at the impassive profile, the gentle smile on his lips as he nodded encouragingly to the patient. Today he was in his consultant's garb of dark suit and crisp white shirt, and could easily have passed for a successful high-flyer in the business world. It was painful to look at him and know that looking was all she *could* do, and her glance once more swept over the students, her eyes quelling two of them who were starting to whisper. If she didn't reprimand them later, Jamie would do so, then blame her for her slackness!

'How long have these compulsions bothered you?' Jamie's voice broke into Linda's thoughts. Of course he was speaking to the patient, but the question, How long have you loved me? might have been more to the point if he had been speaking to her! For she *did* love him, she knew that. And love was a painful experience—only now did she realise just how painful it was.

'Since my—my friend left,' Miss Brent whispered.

'If he came back, would you stop counting and touching things, do you think?' Jamie asked casually, and Miss Brent turned to him, her young-old face brightening as she nodded. She could have been any age, though Linda knew her to be thirty-eight. Of course, even if the man returned, it was unlikely that the compulsions would stop. They had taken such a hold of the woman's life that they wouldn't vanish overnight. If they did, it was possible they would be replaced by some other compulsion, though at the Clinic they weren't finding that the case. Once treatment had banished or subdued the symptoms, they didn't seem to re-occur in another form, which was encouraging.

Miss Brent was the last patient for the round, and once she had gone and the group had discussed her briefly, Linda spoke firmly to the students about their behaviour.

'But it's awfully boring, Sister!' one student complained. 'I mean, it's not a bit like nursing, is it? Just sitting there while some woman talks about her silly behaviour! Surely she could stop it if she tried?'

'I'm sure she would like to stop, but she can't,' Linda explained, being careful not to criticise the student for her opinion. It was an opinion shared by many, lay people as well as general nurses, and Linda felt she had to make the girl understand. 'It's behaviour, silly or not, that's ruining her life. How can she go on with a normal life, get her work done, if she has to keep stopping to touch or count things? If we can help her get back to what we choose to call "normal" behaviour, then surely that's nursing?' she suggested, and the girl nodded reluctantly.

'Yes, I suppose so. I hadn't thought of it quite like that,' she admitted, and Linda smiled, before sending them all to their coffee break. The girls could chew the morning's session over while they had their elevenses, and she wouldn't complain if they took longer than they were allowed. It was better to let them air their opinions—too many hospitals didn't expect learners to even *have* opinions!

'Busy with your little brood, Sister?' A voice spoke in Linda's ear, and she started.

'You frightened me, Dr Grainger!' she said, recovering swiftly. 'I didn't hear you. I——'

'Do I frighten you, Sister? That's an interesting comment,' said Jamie. 'Very revealing.'

'Stop analysing me!' she hissed. 'You don't frighten me at all—just because I told you to save your kisses for Wanda, it doesn't mean I was frightened!'

It was nearly a week since that fateful evening at the barbecue, and beyond the calls of duty she and Jamie had hardly spoken. Once or twice she had seen him eyeing her thoughtfully, but she had avoided him whenever possible and he hadn't sought her out. Of course she was *glad* he hadn't, but even so. . .

'Ah, it's Wanda who has exclusive rights to my kisses, is it?' Jamie chuckled in her ear, and she glared at him. 'Interesting, that,' he went on, then one of the doctors hailed him, and, still chuckling, he ambled away, Linda's puzzled gaze following him. Now what exactly did *that* mean?

It was perhaps as well that they had no opportunity to speak again until late afternoon, when Linda was just about to begin the relaxation classes. Miss Anstey had a half day off work and had been persuaded to attend the relaxation, despite insisting that she didn't need to relax.

'I do enough of that at home, Sister, really!' she assured Linda. 'I don't really think this sort of thing is quite suitable for me,' she went on. 'It's not as if I'm *ill*, is it?'

'No, of course not. Most of our ladies—and gentlemen too—aren't actually ill, they're just the victims of a set of distressing symptoms. That's why they're here,' Linda explained. 'You needn't join in the relaxations if you don't want to, but we do like our people to if they possibly can,' she went on. She had been about to say 'patients' rather than 'people', but as she had just said their clientele weren't actually ill, it was rather a nonsense to call them patients! She really preferred the term 'client' and was determined to have another word with Jamie about it. He was terribly stubborn when he put his mind to it, but she would keep trying!

Relaxation class was an informal affair, and the patients stretched out on thin mattresses laid out on the floor of the exercise room. Miss Anstey, Linda noted, carefully edged her mattress as far away from the others as she could. A difficult lady, that, she reflected, then indicated to Nurse Redmond that she could begin the class. Today Linda herself was going to relax on a mattress while Anne Redmond took over the task of speaking soothingly to the ladies. Sometimes they had a specially made cassette, which played soothing background music while a man spoke about beautiful places in the world, a seascape, perhaps, or a quiet, sunlit meadow with birdsong everywhere—it didn't really matter what he said, Linda often thought, it was the tone of voice, the repetition of certain words, and the music as well. At other times, like today, Linda arranged for a member of staff to speak, with a background of romantic music played very quietly.

She decided to lie next to Miss Anstey, who was clearly relieved. 'I don't like to lie next to anyone I don't know, Sister,' she said in a stage whisper.

Linda smiled at her, then said firmly, 'Now, just lie back, ladies, and Nurse Redmond will send us all to sleep!'

Amid laughter, the ladies settled back, even Miss Anstey, and as far as Linda could see, they had all closed their eyes. She followed suit, and the nurse set the music going. 'Close your eyes, ladies, and pretend a tall, dark and handsome man has just knocked on your back door and asked you out,' Nurse Redmond began, and Linda sat up in surprise. *That* wasn't what she was supposed to say!

Right on cue, Jamie Grainger appeared, and there was a ripple of laughter from the patients. Crossly, Linda got up, wondering what he wanted that couldn't wait.

'Do sit down—or perhaps I should say, *lie* down, Sister Scott,' Jamie said amiably. 'I decided I'd join you today. Is there a mattress for me? Ah, yes, this one will do.' To Linda's astonishment, he selected a spare mattress and brought it over to her. 'May I?' he murmured, not waiting for an answer.

Miss Anstey beamed at him, and obligingly moved up a few inches so that he could lie next to Linda. Nurse Redmond was having one of her giggling fits, and the whole session looked ready to disintegrate into a farce. Wondering whether the nurse had known Jamie was joining in the session, Linda coolly suggested to her that she should begin again. 'Perhaps you could read the passage we agreed on, Staff? *Not* the piece about a tall, dark and handsome man knocking on the back door!'

Anne Redmond giggled again, and Jamie's lips twitched at Linda's obvious discomfiture, but she refused to be put off, merely settled herself on the mattress, keeping as far to the left as she could, nearer the patient than to Jamie, and determinedly closed her eyes, hoping the patients would settle down again and that the entire session hadn't been ruined. It was an important part of the treatment as far as she was concerned. Phobic people, particularly, needed to be put into a relaxed frame of mind before they could begin their treatment programme.

This time, Nurse Redmond read out the selection of

poems Linda had chosen. Her voice had dropped a little, and Linda thought she handled the session well, her words flowing over the group, so much so that Linda almost dropped off. She was weary, anyway, and with all the emotion raging around her life at the moment she was as much in need of relaxation as any of the patients. Even the fact that Jamie was lying on a mattress next to her didn't keep her awake, but she heard his soft chuckle.

'Enjoying yourself, Sister?' he asked lazily, as the nurse paused, but Linda wouldn't give him the satisfaction of knowing just how much she would have enjoyed lying next to him for real!

At last the relaxations were over, and none too soon for her peace of mind. Several of the ladies came over to tell her how much they had enjoyed it, and she made a point of seeing that the nurse got her fair share of praise, but it rankled that Nurse Redmond knew more about Jamie's movements than she did herself.

'You didn't tell me you were joining in today, Doctor,' she said smoothly, and he shrugged.

'Would it have made any difference? You seem to be avoiding me, so I told the only nurse I could find—Staff Nurse Redmond,' he said affably. 'Have you been avoiding me? Or is it just a strange fancy I have?' he went on. His body was blocking her only escape route and Linda didn't know what to say. The patients had left the room, and the nurse was busy with the cassette player in a corner, apparently not listening to them, but Linda couldn't be sure of that.

'No, of course I haven't, Doctor,' she said quietly. 'I've been preoccupied, I suppose, what with one thing and another. Do you want me to see Mrs Skilton tomorrow?' she hurried on, and Jamie smiled wryly.

'Yes, Mrs Skilton. How are things going along there?' he asked, and Linda walked with him along the corridor to his office while they discussed the agoraphobic patient.

'She's a bit better, I think, but she needs an exhaustive session of treatment,' Linda ventured. 'Now we've persuaded her husband to show a bit of sympathy and encourage her instead of criticising, she's making some headway, but not enough.'

Jamie nodded, his brooding gaze on her face. They stopped outside his office door and Linda waited, uneasily aware that her expression might reveal more than she intended. 'I keep telling the money men we need a nurse-therapist,' he commented, 'and I intend to have one next year—though you seem to be combining both jobs,' he pointed out.

Not sure if he was criticising her for exceeding her duties, Linda agreed that they needed a full-time nurse-therapist, someone who could take Mrs Skilton safely through the various stages of treatment. 'I'm seeing her twice a week, and we're working through the programme you gave her, but she still keeps hinting about being admitted.'

'That's definitely out of the question,' he began, then stood aside for her to enter his office. That wasn't what she had intended at all, and she stopped, but unfortunately so did he, and somehow their bodies touched, his nearness sending her nervous system into panic stations!

'You flinched then, Sister,' Jamie said stonily. 'Does my presense upset you that much?'

'No, no, of course it doesn't! I mean, no, you don't! You get me so confused sometimes, I don't know *what* I mean!' flared Linda, aware that she was being unreasonable.

'Do I confuse you?' Jamie drawled, a wicked gleam in his eye. 'Now why is that, I wonder?'

She opened her mouth to tell him, then closed it again. 'Excuse me, Doctor, but I have some reports to type.'

Jamie's smile was wolfish, and Linda thankfully escaped, her face burning.

The phone rang just as she reached her own office. Unfortunately it was Paul, and although she kept the conversation brief, it was only seconds before a stern-faced Jamie materialised.

'I'll have to hang up now—see you later, Paul. Enjoy your revising!' she said lightly, then put the receiver down, waiting for her chief to make some acidic comment.

'At least he's got something to revise,' was all the comment Jamie made. 'It proves he's capable of working at something, anyway.'

'Yes, it does. He isn't *all* bad. I know he's a pain sometimes, but he *has* been ill, and——'

'He isn't ill, Linda, he's got a personality defect. Rather like Chrissie, I'm afraid,' Jame went on wearily. He stood over by the window, but his eyes were on her.

Linda knew that to be the truth, but stubbornly refused to admit it to him. 'He is ill, or has been. That's why he was at the Baxter. His girlfriend died and he developed reactive depression.'

'Perfectly normal in the circumstances, I should have thought. I don't belong to the school of thought that considers reactive depression as a mental illness or in any way abnormal. Depression after the death of a loved one is what one would expect, surely?'

Reluctantly, Linda nodded her agreement. Jamie half turned his back on her, appearing to find the view from the window more interesting. Then he swung round suddenly, catching her feasting her eyes on him, and hastily she glanced down at her desk.

There was a sheaf of notes there and she picked them up, just for something to do with her hands. 'Oh, Linda!' he breathed, then stopped, causing her to glance up again. There was something very like anguish in his eyes, then abruptly the shutters came down again.

Perhaps fortunately, Nurse Craig popped her head around the door to say goodnight, and Linda was able to escape. Shaken, she crossed to her car, wondering for how much longer she could stay at the Clinic, knowing as she did just how much she cared for Jamie Grainger. It wasn't fair to him, or to Wanda. Nor was it good for her to spend nearly every day with him, knowing that he was unobtainable. One way or another, something had to give!

'Linda! Surprise, surprise!'

Linda whirled round, her eyes widening at the sound of a familiar voice from the past. She paused long enough for Tim Coleman to catch up and he fell into step with her, his face animated.

'This *is* a surprise,' Linda smiled. 'I thought you were still at the Baxter? You haven't come to join the Summerheath, have you?'

Tim shook his head, then rubbed a large hand ruefully against his chin, where yesterday's stubble still showed. 'As a matter of fact, I overslept this morning. Sorry about the trendy vagrant look! Still, it isn't likely I'll see the Big White Chief, is it? Being Saturday, and all.'

'I never know when he's going to turn up,' Linda admitted. 'As a matter of fact, I don't usually work on a Saturday, but we can't tell patients not to become ill at weekends just because it's inconvenient for us! Jamie—

Dr Grainger—has agreed that I might start a weekend clinic, so I'm hoping to start next Saturday.'

'Jamie, is it? From what I saw of him, I'm amazed you're on first-name terms!' Tim waited, but Linda made no comment, nor did she do so as he followed her into her office. The other day patient staff weren't about, her only nursing company being the staff of the in-patient unit, and she waved to the sister on duty before settling herself beside her desk and waving her former colleague to a seat.

'It's been a long time—no, I suppose it hasn't,' she began. 'It only *seems* a long time! I feel as if I've been at the Summerheath for ages.' She smiled to herself, and Tim had to whistle softly to regain her attention.

'Hello, Sister Scott! I'm still here!' he grinned, and she waved her fist at him.

'Sorry, I'm a bit preoccupied these days. You heard that Paul Winterton moved in with me, I suppose?' Tim had been Paul's charge nurse at the Baxter, and probably knew him better than anyone else.

'I heard, yes. From young Paul's own lips, incidentally—he was at the Baxter looking up old friends a while back. I warned him not to be a nuisance to you, but he just smiled. You know that innocent little smile he has!'

'Yes, only too well,' Linda said with some asperity. 'I can't get rid of him, but at least he's getting on with his book now——'

'Book!' scoffed Tim. 'He'll never finish it! He's never finished anything, no matter what it is!'

'But he will!' she protested. 'He's nearly finished now, and I do his typing. I'm getting a bit sick of it, to be frank! Still, when he's in a good mood, he's pleasant company, and I think once he *does* finish the book he'll drift away. He's starting to disappear for days at a time.'

'Mm—well, I hope you're right.' Tim sounded doubtful, then leaned on her desk and smiled at her. 'Anyway, enough about patients—tell me what you'd like to do at the weekend and I'll pull out all the stops! How about a trip on the Bluebell Railway? I read about it somewhere. Or——'

'I enjoy historical sights, Tim, but I'm taking some of the ladies to see Arundel Castle shortly, and all I really want to do on my weekends off is sleep.' She tried to smile, but it didn't really come off, and Tim gave her a thoughtful look.

Once she and Tim had been good friends. There was a possibility, even, that they might have become more than that, but somehow things hadn't worked out. They remained friends, enjoyed sightseeing, long walks, fresh air, but that was all. Still, an evening out with Tim would make a welcome change—at least she could talk to him, as long as she didn't talk about a certain consultant psychiatrist! 'Dinner one evening would be nice,' she ventured, and Tim brightened visibly.

'Yes, wouldn't it? Right you are—how about tonight? Saturday night on the town!' He beamed at her, and she hadn't the heart to tell him she wanted the evening to herself.

'That would be lovely,' she said instead. 'It's about time I had an evening out with a handsome young man!' she added, laughing, and Tim chuckled. It was true— Tim *was* good-looking, in a healthy, outdoor way, with a mass of blond curls bleached almost white by the sun, large violet-blue eyes, and a direct way of looking at people that Linda found arresting. Yes, it would be good for her, and they could at least talk shop.

'Why aren't you having a bit more social life?' he asked frankly, and, surprised, she shrugged.

'You know how it is—work, work, and yet more work!'

'All work and no play isn't good for Sister Scott! You ought to get out and about more, let the hordes of eager young men wine and dine you,' Tim said firmly. 'What about Paul? I know he's too damn selfish to take you out, but is there a budding romance there?'

Linda shook her head firmly, the fine fair hair swishing about her face. 'No, definitely not! Paul can't understand it. He thinks he's God's gift to women and that I must find him utterly irresistible!' He wasn't the only man who thought that either, she added silently. 'I can't feel anything for him other than friendship, and even that's wearing a bit thin these days!' she said lightly. 'A little of Paul goes a long way and I was a fool to let him stay, but what could I do? He got my address from someone at the Baxter, then turned up at the cottage one lunch-time, so pleased to see me, so grateful that I let him stay to lunch, and—well——' She paused. 'You know the rest—one lunch stretched to half a dozen, and he's still here!'

'You'll have to chuck him out, Linda. Do you want me to do it for you?' Tim looked as if he would relish the job, but Linda refused.

'No, water will find its own level, as they say—once the book's on its travels, he'll take off somewhere.'

'But will he return? That's what you've got to guard against. If he does come back, let me know—will you?' Tim's kind eyes smiled at her, and Linda nodded. It was good to know she'd got at least *one* friend, someone she could rely on.

'I suppose if the worst came to the worst, I could

always leave, go home for a while,' she said thoughtfully, 'but I like it here. I really enjoy the challenge. . .' Yes, she did, but Dr Jamie Grainger was too much of a challenge sometimes, and she thought there would be an explosion some time, the only question was *when*!

'I'll pick you up around seven tonight, shall I? Oh, you'd better give me directions—I tried to find your cottage but got stuck at a level crossing and lost my sense of direction after that! You certainly believe in rural hideaways.'

'It isn't that bad!' Linda protested. 'I know about the level crossing—Jamie showed me a short cut from here to the cottage, so I can avoid the crossing now. He——'

'Ah, yes, Jamie,' said Tim, a strange expression on his face. 'You keep mentioning him—that's why I'm here, anyway. He's giving a few of us a tour around the Clinic on Monday, and I've come down first to look you up. I'm glad I did,' he added, with a meaning look, but Linda pretended not to notice.

'He didn't tell me, but we——' She paused. She could hardly tell Tim that she and Jamie were avoiding each other! He might wonder why, and being a perceptive man, he wouldn't take long to work *that* one out! 'I haven't seen much of him lately,' she said instead. 'He's so busy, and we could do with more nursing staff. The Clinic and what we do for the patients was mentioned on the radio a few weeks back—just before I came—and referrals have come flooding in! We can't keep pace.'

'It's surprising the number of people who need help, just a little help in most cases,' Tim acknowledged. 'I'd better let you get on, I suppose—unless there's anything I can do? You've no patients this morning, I suppose?'

Linda shook her head. 'No, I'm trying to spend part of the morning phoning around, trying to get people interested in coming next Saturday, or any Saturday, come to that. We'll see how it goes from there. You can stay, though. There's no need to rush away—unless you'd like to go back to the cottage? I can lend you my key,' she offered.

'You're a sweet, trusting little soul, Linda Scott— mind I don't take advantage of you,' he said quietly, then dropped a kiss on her brow. 'The dreadful Paul won't be there, will he?'

'No, he's gone to his sister for a couple of days. I'm having a ham salad for lunch—you can prepare it, if you like. The seasoning's in the cupboard by the back door and everything else is in the fridge,' she told him, and a happy Tim went off, brandishing her key for all to see.

All it needed was for Jamie to walk through the door! Linda mused, then turned at a sound from the corridor leading to the in-patient unit. Sister Whitehead, the ward sister, stood there, an uncertain smile on her face.

'Sorry—I hope I didn't interrupt anything! Only you've got some notes on agoraphobia in here, and Jamie said I might borrow them, if that's all right?' she went on, her sharp gaze on Linda, who felt acutely uncomfortable.

Wondering how much the other sister had seen, Linda handed her the notes she had been using, but even when she was alone again, the uncomfortable feeling persisted. Sister Whitehead must have seen her hand the key to Tim! And what sort of interpretation would she put on *that*? Linda wondered for the rest of the morning.

She was able to contact seven of the ten names on her list, and those who lived alone were keen on attending some weekends. For some of them it was tantamount to a treat, Linda thought sadly. At least at the Clinic, they were among people who understood their symptoms. It might be a good idea to ask a discharged patient along occasionally just to let the current patients see that their symptoms *could* be alleviated, and that they would, one day, lead the normal life they had once enjoyed. Yes, she would have to see Jamie about that.

In fact, there were so many things she had to see Jamie about that a long meeting with him was inevitable the following week. It was silly, anyway, trying to avoid her chief. Surely they could act like sensible, mature adults and not let their personal animosity get in the way of their professional duties? They owed it to the patients, if not to the rest of the staff, Linda decided firmly. On Monday she would begin.

CHAPTER EIGHT

'AND a hairdresser?' Linda ventured on the Monday, after she had waylaid Jamie in his office. 'That's something most of the ladies would appreciate, and we could even include the men. They——'

'Whoa!' Jamie said softly, a reluctant smile tugging at his mouth. 'You're so full of schemes, Sister Scott, but where's the money coming from?—that's the number one question in this place. Secondly, we have to consider how many patients would take advantage of the facility. Thirdly whether we charge them, or try to take the strain ourselves. Fourthly——' he went on relentlessly, and Linda jumped to her feet, exasperated.

He had done nothing except pour cold water on all her ideas this morning! Anyone would think he didn't *want* her to have a mind of her own! 'I'm sorry if my enthusiasm is running away with me,' she said crossly, 'but you were the one who said it was good to have a keen day patient sister. You said——'

'Sit down, Linda. I feel like a naughty schoolboy when you stand there breathing fire all over me!' Jamie said gently, and a flushed Linda did as she was bid.

'I'm sorry, but you—you. . .' She stopped, knowing it was no use. He really could be irritating when he put himself out!

Jamie leaned back in his chair, his eyes half closed, a satisfied little smile on his mouth, and Linda had the urge to—well, she didn't know what exactly, perhaps kiss him, if she was honest about it. Oh, Jamie! her heart

cried. Hastily veiling her giveaway expression, she tried
again. Remember you're a sensible, mature adult, she
told herself. What happened to Saturday morning's good
resolutions? 'Dr Grainger,' she began, and Jamie sat up,
steepling his fingers and trying to look serious.

Yes, Sister, what is it?' he said solemnly, and Linda
smiled involuntarily. 'Yes, that's better,' he went on. 'A
smile a day keeps the shrink away! Haven't you ever
heard that expression, Sister?' He smiled into her eyes,
and Linda hastily glanced down at her sheaf of notes.
She had intended to ask him so much, but not when he
was in this sort of mood!

'I'll try to remember that, Dr Grainger,' she said
soothingly. 'Now, about the hairdresser. . .'

He sighed, then ran his fingers through his hair.
'You're a nag, Sister Scott, that's what you are. But I'll
see what can be done,' he agreed. 'The Clinic *does* have
a budget, though, and I have to see that we can stay
within that budget,' he pointed out. 'Our dear Admin
officer keeps coming up with ways of getting more value
out of every pound we spend, and I don't know how
he'll view the purchase price of a hairdresser. These
money men see things differently, Linda.'

'I know, I know, but you will try, won't you?' Linda
leaned forward, her eyes willing him to help get her
schemes off the ground, but it had the opposite effect.
Jamie's eyes hardened, and she wondered what was
coming next.

'I'll see what I can do,' he said dismissively. 'Now, on
to other things—the group from the Baxter this afternoon. I meant to tell you, but, what with one thing and
another. . . Anyway, you know at least one of the nurses,
I take it?'

He raised a brow interrogatively, and Linda chose her

words carefully before replying. He was beginning to resemble Paul in that respect—take out each word and turn it over before emitting it! 'Yes, I know Tim Coleman, if that's who you mean. He came into the Clinic on Saturday—we lunched together,' some little imp made her add.

'Not forgetting dinner,' Jamie said stonily, and her eyes widened.

'Yes, he *did* take me out to dinner, but where were you? I didn't see you anywhere!' She felt betrayed.

'I was at home, enjoying a solitary meal, actually,' Jamie admitted coolly. 'Wanda saw you and rang me, asked me who the handsome man was. She thought it might be Winterton.'

'Oh, did she?' Linda said weakly. 'I didn't see her in the restaurant. Was she with a group of friends? There was a group by the river—oh!' Yes, she remembered now, the little group had included Jenny Meacham, she had spotted that extraordinary red hair from right across the room! 'She must have been with that noisy group,' she said slowly.

'Was it noisy? I imagine it was, with the Meachams there.' Jamie gave a wry smile. 'Wanda enjoyed herself, that's the important thing.'

'I'm glad,' Linda said simply. 'I enjoyed myself too,' she added, though she wanted to bite back the words the moment she had spoken. Why torment herself by telling lies to Jamie? *He* wouldn't care one way or the other.

'Did you enjoy your lunch as well?' Jamie demanded, taking her aback. He got up and began pacing restlessly up and down his office. Luckily it was larger than hers, but he was still too big for it, and her eyes followed his movements—so much leashed energy to be caged.

'Yes, well, we didn't go out to lunch,' she admitted,

talking to his back, for Jamie was hunched over at the window, head bowed, broad back firm and unyielding. Linda had the absurd desire to cry, but only patients were allowed that sort of liberty in front of the consultant psychiatrist!

'Is he an ex-lover? Or without the ex?' he asked at last, still with his back turned, and Linda gasped.

'Tim? No, hardly that! We were just—friends at the Baxter, that's all. I suppose we might have drifted into a romance,' she went on thoughtfully, wondering if that was so, but since she didn't feel any emotional stirrings when Tim was around, she thought it unlikely. Paul didn't arouse her in that way either, and she sometimes thought she must be abnormal—at least she *had* thought that, until she met Jamie Grainger and experienced all the strange yearnings that love brought. As far as Jamie was concerned, she was definitely normal enough!

'Perhaps you will now—once you've got rid of young Winterton,' Jamie suggested, then turned to face her. 'I don't want to make an issue of it, Linda, but I've asked you before to keep your private life under wraps. If you *must* give your key to all and sundry, at least do so when you're off duty!'

'How dare you! I didn't. . .' Linda stopped, for clearly she *had* given Tim the key, she could hardly deny it. 'I lent Tim my key so he could prepare the lunch for me. I worked all Saturday morning,' she added tautly. Her nerves were at breaking point, and she knew how some of the patients felt—for most of them it was a case of 'grin and bear it', with their family and friends often not understanding their problems. She had no one to understand hers, either. Her mother was too far away, and anyway, Mum wouldn't have understood how working in close proximity with someone like Jamie Grainger could become wearing. Now that Mum had recovered from her own unhappy marriage, it wasn't fair to burden her with minor worries.

'Yes, I know you worked,' said Jamie, more gently. 'I'm afraid we can't pay you any overtime, but take time off during the week to make up—that darned budget again!' he joked, but his voice sounded strained, and Linda wanted to go over and comfort him.

'Perhaps I can add it to my holiday—I had a week arranged for August, but I can alter it if you want me to?' she offered.

'No, keep that week. We'll get by somehow.' Jamie was gazing out of the window again, and Linda couldn't tell by the tone of his voice exactly what he'd meant. She suspected a hint of sarcasm, but couldn't be sure. Well, of course they would manage. Hadn't they managed without her for the three years the Clinic had been operating? No, Jamie wouldn't miss her. Why should he?

'You really ought to get away for a holiday, Linda.' Jamie yawned and stretched, the muscles rippling under the thin shirt he wore, and abruptly she picked up a copy of a nursing magazine and pretended to study it.

'I nearly did, but the girl I was going with lost her mother—we were going to Rome, but maybe another year. By the way, there's an article I wanted to ask you about.' Linda waved the magazine at him. 'It's a case history of an agoraphobic,' she went on in a rush, not wanting to discuss Tim, Paul *or* the episode of the key again. 'It reminded me of Gwen Skilton. This patient here——' She rapidly turned the pages, trying to find the one she sought.

Jame was beside her as she reached it. 'Here—it's a two-page article. I suppose you haven't read it?' She knew she was gabbling, but his nearness was unsettling, to put it mildly! What a fool he must think her. At least with Wanda he knew where he was. Wanda *was* mature and practical, sensible, warm and loving too, Linda supposed sadly.

'Yes, I *have* read it. I read all the nursing magazines, and there seem to be a great many of them these days! I like to keep up with nursing techniques as well as medical ones,' he said gently, turning her to face him.

Linda tried to still the trembling in her limbs, but wasn't entirely successful. 'Don't tell me you're cold?' Jamie said tenderly, then put out his hand and stroked her hair. 'Such pretty hair—you must make the other nurses green with envy!' he chuckled, and she relaxed a little. At least he was in a good mood again.

'I keep thinking about cutting it, but——' She broke off. It was no business of his, and of no interest to him either.

'Yes, why not? It'll be cooler for the summer, but don't cut it too short, Linda. Your hair's lovely as it is,' he added, and Linda shot him a puzzled glance.

'Several compliments at one go!' she said shakily, and that mulish expression crossed Jamie's face again.

'Put it down to the hot weather!' he suggested, then picked up the magazine she had indicated, and the moment of togetherness was lost. Linda shivered a little, then hurriedly fished in her bag for her gold pen.

Jamie noticed. 'That pen again—is it special?' He sounded annoyed, and she wondered why.

Reluctantly, she held out the pen for his inspection. 'Yes, it's a Parker—it was my father's—he died several years ago and about the only item of value he left was this pen. He drank,' she said simply, then hastily stuffed it away, snapped her bag closed and hurried to the door, not waiting for Jamie's protestations of sympathy, kind words. She didn't want any of those things, for heaven's sake! She wanted Jamie Grainger—and what Linda wanted, yet again Linda couldn't have.

'Linda.' Jamie's voice halted her at the door, and she spun round to face him, her expression set, her eyes cool. Being the daughter of a drunkard was bad enough, without people commiserating. It was all over now, and if anyone deserved pity, it was Mum.

'I didn't know, but we won't talk of it again. Sit down and tell me about the article—were you thinking of writing one? If Winterton's got printer's ink in his veins, perhaps some of it's spread to you,' he went on, and Linda gasped.

'If that remark means what I think it does——' she began hotly, then a husky chuckle from behind her sent her whirling around. Wanda stood there, in a multi-coloured caftan, her eyes going from one to the other.

'I *do* apologise—I'd no idea I was interrupting a quarrel,' Wanda laughed, 'but Muriel Craig said I should come straight in. I hope that's all right, Jamie?'

'Yes, of course. Come in, Wanda.' An obviously distracted Jamie waved a hand towards a chair, and Linda took the opportunity to escape, but didn't quite make it.

'Don't let me stop you, my dear,' said Wanda, putting her hand on Linda's arm. Her eyes were sympathetic, but that was the last thing Linda wanted.

'I was just going. I'm afraid Jamie and I were arguing over the budget again!' She forced herself to speak lightly. 'Good old money problems!' Still smiling, she at last made her escape, hoping Wanda wouldn't notice that one tear had escaped her tight control and was making its lonely way down her cheek.

Before she closed the door, she heard Wanda say, 'Jamie! How could you? I told you there was——' Then she was out of earshot, and would never know what it was Wanda had told him. Whatever it was, it didn't matter. Nothing mattered any more.

It was Linda who had the job of showing the Baxter Clinic nurses around that afternoon, and to her dismay, Tim stayed close beside her. She knew most of the nurses, anyway, and one ward sister in particular was, she knew, fond of Tim, and she felt awful at the way he ignored the girl.

'Tim,' she said firmly as they sat down to afternoon tea in the canteen, 'you'll have to stay with the group. You haven't spoken one word to Pam since you arrived!'

He shrugged. 'I can talk to her any time, I hardly see *you* any more. Anyway, there's nothing between us— except what her vivid imagination conjures up! Tell me again how much you enjoyed our evening out,' he encouraged.

She *had* enjoyed dining with him, in an olde-worlde inn by the river. Yet how much more she would have enjoyed it if her companion had been Jamie Grainger! Her face clouded and Tim leaned forward, all concern, his hand resting gently on hers. It was that moment Jamie chose to put in an appearance, and Linda watched his tall figure stride across to their table.

'Sorry I couldn't get away before, folks,' he apologised with one of his charming smiles, 'but I'm sure Sister Scott has been entertaining you.' His sharp glance took in the intimate gesture Tim had made, and Linda felt like snatching her hand away, but wouldn't give Jamie that pleasure. He had no right to keep making insinuations about her personal life—there he was with a lover years older than himself. He made no attempt to hide Wanda or disguise her status, so he ought not to sit in judgement on others.

Face flushed, Linda sat there, hardly listening to what Jamie was saying. Then Tim grinned and clapped her on the back, and she turned her startled gaze on him.

Jamie's smile was grim, and there was an ominous gleam in his eyes. 'I don't believe Sister has been listening to us—have you, Sister Scott?'

Discomfited, Linda shook her head. 'I'm sorry, no, my mind was miles away!' she admitted with a little laugh. He didn't miss a thing!

'Never mind, my pet,' Tim said fondly. 'Dr Grainger won't mind my telling you—he was saying what an enthusiastic day patient sister you are, and that the Baxter's loss is the Summerheath's gain!'

There was a smattering of applause from the other nurses, and Linda didn't know where to put her face. Praise indeed! 'Thank you, ladies and gentlemen,' she said, avoiding Jamie's gaze.

'And for her next trick——' Tim began, amid more laughter. Even Jamie joined in, and Linda heaved a sigh of relief, though whether he would take her to task later on was another matter. He might consider they were enjoying themselves too much and that it wasn't professional. Well, just let him tell *her* that!

The tour of the Clinic concluded with the group joining in the relaxations, and, mindful of the last time Jamie had joined in, Linda was careful to position herself between two patients, well away from him.

Anne Redmond did the honours, and Linda was quick to thank her afterwards. 'Thank you, Sister!' The nurse beamed. 'What with Dr Grainger praising me and now you, I won't be able to get through the door for my swollen head!'

Linda saw the group off, promising to write to Tim every now and then. 'Just so I can see that you're all right,' he said. 'And let me know if you have any trouble with our friend Paul,' he added, squeezing her hand as they left.

She still had a smile on her face as she walked slowly back towards her office, but was waylaid by Mrs Ellershaw, who had lingered behind once the other patients had left. 'I just wanted to say how much I enjoyed the relaxations, Sister. Well, the company more, I suppose,' Mrs Ellershaw admitted.

'That's what you need—company,' Linda told her. 'Dr Grainger was saying that you're obviously lonely,' she went on, and the woman's face brightened.

'*Was* he? Does he talk about me?' she asked eagerly.

'Of course. We discuss all the patients—two heads are better than one!' Linda assured her. 'I expect you're missing your friends from home?'

Mrs Ellershaw seemed about to deny this, then agreed that she did. 'I come from Leicester originally, but my late husband travelled a lot and naturally I travelled with him. We had no family, so we could please ourselves, really. It's years since I was back home—I haven't any roots anywhere, and that's a fact.' She stood waiting, and Linda didn't quite know what was expected of her. The obvious thing to do was invite her home, perhaps to tea one day, make a friend of her, but that was something she was strictly forbidden to do. Jamie had made a point of telling her that at the interview—don't get too involved in the private lives of the patients. Apart from the fact that a nurse needed her off-duty, needed to get away from patients and even other nurses, such interest didn't do the patient any good in the long run. Encouraging dependence upon hospital staff simply wasn't on. Linda knew the truth of that—many times she wished she hadn't let Paul move in. She had broken the unwritten rule and was now paying for it. If she encouraged Mrs Ellershaw, such was that lady's personality that she might never be able to shake her off completely, no matter how much it would be to the patient's benefit.

So she merely smiled and suggested that some voluntary work might be a good idea. 'Help the local hospital—that sort of work is very rewarding,' Linda encouraged, 'and you'd soon make new friends that way. If you attend here once a week, you'll soon get to know the other ladies as well,' she pointed out, and Mrs Ellershaw looked disappointed.

'I don't know as I want to get to know the others, to be frank, Sister—some of them seem very wrapped up in themselves. Still, I'll make the best of it. Thank you for sparing the time to talk to me—I know how hard you people work!' With a cheery wave, she walked quickly away, leaving Linda feeling ashamed that she hadn't been more forthcoming. Surely inviting her to tea just *once* wouldn't be breaking the Clinic rule?

Sadly, she continued on her way, and wasn't aware of Jamie until a whiff of aftershave alerted her. He was leaning against the door of the interview-room, clearly waiting for her. She stopped, her expression grave. 'Do you realise the trouble your rules and regulations cause, Dr Grainger?' she asked quietly, determined to get her piece in before he began on his usual criticisms of her. 'Poor Mrs Ellershaw's desperately lonely, and I would have liked to invite her to——'

'No!' Jamie made a chopping motion with his hand, and, affronted, Linda closed her mouth. There was no point in trying to tell him he was wrong—he was never wrong!

If she thought she might escape, she was mistaken, and an irate Jamie opened the door wider, silently inviting her in. It was too much, and, stubbornly, she refused. Head held high, she defied him. The man couldn't eat her, for heaven's sake! She was being a coward letting him get away with ordering her about. 'Some rules are made to be broken!' she retorted, surprising herself as well as him. 'I could have asked her to tea, or taken her for a drive—where's the harm in that?' she challenged, and a little smile hovered about Jamie's mouth.

'Paul Winterton,' he said softly. 'That's my answer. You took *him* under your wing and look where it got you! Don't get involved with patients *or* people with personality defects, Linda. It isn't worth ruining your life as well as theirs. Mrs Ellershaw is a perfectly normal woman, and once she's got over her bout of guilt feelings, she'll make friends and go her own way. She isn't ill, she just needs a bit of support and——'

'That's just what I've been saying!' Linda protested hotly. 'If *we* don't support her, who will? Surely it's up to us to do more for patients? We could——'

'No, no, no!' Jamie thundered, then grasped her firmly by the arm and marched her into the room. He closed the door behind them, then stood with his back to it, breathing heavily. Resentfully, she waited. Whatever Jamie said, she wouldn't change her views, and he was wasting his valuable time trying to make her.

A reluctant smile touched his mouth, then was gone. 'Sometimes I feel like shaking you until you see sense, Linda Scott,' he said mildly enough. 'At other times,' he went on, moving nearer, 'you talk a lot of sense and I wonder whether *I'm* the one at fault.' The smile came back, those light eyes smiling into hers, and Linda was momentarily thrown.

'I—well, thank you,' she managed. 'I'm surprised to hear you admit you're ever at fault,' she couldn't resist adding, and his smile faded.

'Psychiatrists are people who keep their emotions well under control,' he said tightly, still looking down at her, and she nodded silently. 'So either I'm the exception to the rule—and I don't believe I am—or *you* are to blame for my constantly losing my temper. Now, which is it, hm?'

Linda squirmed under his scrutiny. Unwilling to take the blame for what must, after all, be mostly his fault, she ventured, 'I might be partly to blame, I suppose— but not entirely,' she added firmly. 'No way am I acting as whipping boy for the faults in *your* personality!'

'Ah, that's better—the old Sister Scott back again!' he chuckled. 'I thought for a moment I'd succeeded in taming you!'

'I dare say there are faults on both sides,' Linda admitted coolly. 'Now, please may I return to my office? I've rather a lot of paperwork to see to.'

Ignoring her request, Jamie indicated her suit. 'I like that colour. What is it? Puce? No, maroon, I think.' He came towards her as if to inspect the colour, and Linda held up a hand.

'It's neither puce nor maroon, Dr Grainger. It's meant to be burgundy—I'm not sure it's quite the right colour for a blonde, though. I suppose I should stick to pastels,' she went on quickly, anxious to get away.

'I dislike pale, tacky colours,' Jamie said firmly. '*This* blonde should continue to wear bright, happy colours.

It's good for the patients, not to mention the psychiatrist!'

Linda murmured her thanks, determined not to throw *that* compliment back in his face. 'Now may I go?' she asked sweetly.

'Yes, if you must—but only if you let me take you out to dinner one evening this week.'

She halted in surprise. 'Oh! That's very kind of you, but——'

Jamie misinterpreted her hesitation, for he said, 'Of course, I'd forgotten Winterton, not to mention Charge Nurse Coleman. You're in great demand now. Which of them is wining and dining you this week?'

He sounded so offhand that Linda could have cried. 'Well, I don't know, both of them, probably. But I thought—what about Wanda? Should you be taking your staff out to dinner? Doesn't she feel put out?'

'Put out? Should she be?' Jamie's eyes narrowed. 'What relationship do you suppose Wanda and I enjoy?'

Taken aback, Linda didn't know what to say. 'I should have thought it was obvious, Dr Grainger,' she said coldly. 'Now I really must get on—but if you change your mind about my inviting Mrs Ellershaw to tea, I'd be grateful if you'd let me know,' she added formally, then left, not glancing back. What an extraordinary question about Wanda! As if it wasn't obvious that they were lovers!

'It makes a change to have a male patient, anyway,' Anne Redmond commented a few days later, reading from the referral form Linda handed to her.

'I know. I suppose we're geared mainly to women,' Linda said thoughtfully. 'It isn't true to say that men don't have compulsions, though, and they certainly get depressed. This man is.' She indicated the form. 'Dr Grainger picked him up at Outpatients' Clinic at the General.' Like many, Mr Staplehurst thought his symptoms were something to be ashamed of, a dreadful thing to be hidden, but now at last he'd had to bring them out into the open. Apart from a compulsion to keep washing his hands, he had developed a fear of leaving a window open somewhere and encouraging burglars.

'I see he's got the burglar syndrome,' Nurse Redmond put in, as she finished reading. 'We had a patient like that at my last hospital. She thought burglars were trying to get into the house, even in broad daylight, and it took months to get her rid of the idea.'

'This man has a valid reason for his fears,' Linda put in. 'His office *was* broken into some while back, and someone at the office *did* leave the window unbolted. It wasn't him, but he was responsible for checking the windows, and it seems odd that he missed that one. People like that are over-conscientious, if anything. Poor Miss Anstey keeps believing she's handing out more money to her customers at the bank than they ought to have! She's convinced she's giving away millions of the bank's money, whereas her till is usually correct. There seems no end to it,' Linda sighed, then picked up all the papers on her desk and gave them to the nurse. 'If you wouldn't mind filing these for me, I'll get on with this report. Doctor wants to see Mr Staplehurst here as soon as possible—the CPN's going to bring him in, but I'd like to get the paperwork out of the way before I go.'

'Right you are, Sister—oh, is it all right if I go a bit earlier tonight? Only I've got a date and I don't want to keep him waiting. You know what men are like!'

Surprised, Linda nodded. 'Yes, of course. Just file

that lot away, or do as much as you've time for, then off you go! Have a good evening.'

Linda had nearly finished the report by the time the nurse left, then Muriel Craig poked her head around the door. 'Did you say Anne could leave early! She's just gone.' There was disapproval in every line of the older nurse.

'Yes, she's got a date, so I said she might go when she'd finished. Did she leave something undone? Don't worry about it—I'll finish it if you want to get away.' Nurse Craig had a husband and two sons to cater for, so Linda liked to see she got away at a reasonable hour.

'A date? So that's what she calls it!' Nurse Craig sniffed. 'I saw her getting into our Jamie's car a few minutes ago, and away they went. Wanda won't like that. Well, I'll be off, then—don't stay too long, Sister. 'Bye!'

Linda stared at the open doorway, listening to Nurse Craig's rubber-soled shoes as she padded away. *Wanda won't like that*. Linda Scott didn't like it much either, but unlike Wanda, she had no right to object.

CHAPTER NINE

'COME IN, Linda. Make yourself at home!' Wanda laughed, as she showed Linda into the spacious sitting-room at the front of Jamie's house. 'Just let me tidy a few things away,' she went on, sweeping a pile of sewing off one chair, then, to Linda's surprise, shooing a big black cat off the settee. It gazed at them both in astonishment then stalked off.

'Now I've upset him,' grinned Wanda. 'Here, sit on the chair and I'll take Fluffy's seat. He's kept it warm!' she trilled, obviously in high good humour, and a pensive Linda sat down, wondering whether this was the calm before the storm. It was possible that Wanda would burst into tears at any moment because of Jamie's infidelity, and Linda didn't know quite what she would do if that happened. Of course, if she wasn't emotionally involved herself, she would take it all in her stride, but as it was. . .

'How are you feeling?' she ventured. 'You certainly seem in top form!'

'Mm, I am! I feel so well now that I'm going home next week. Of course I shall miss Jamie, but Fluffy and I want our own home—there's nothing like your own hearth, is there?' Wanda smiled across at her, then, apparently not expecting any comment, she went on, 'Jamie tells me you're taking some of the patients to Arundel at the end of the month—isn't that wonderful? You must all come and have tea with me afterwards.'

Linda hesitated, mindful of Jamie's rules and regulations, then put them firmly out of her mind. 'Yes, that would be lovely. I'm sure the ladies will be happy to accept. We're going to the Castle, then perhaps a quick look around the town, if there's time.'

'There's quite a lot to see in Arundel,' Wanda told her. 'Now, tell me how you and Jamie are getting along. It seems to me you're getting along like a house on fire—someone has to call the fire brigade!' Wanda laughed at her own joke, and Linda joined in, but it was hard trying to pretend it was a joking matter. Wanda's remark was only too true!

'We get along reasonably well,' she said cautiously, since Wanda seemed to be expecting an answer of some sort. 'Naturally, we have our differences.'

'Yes, you would, wouldn't you?' Wanda commented. 'Too much alike, that's the matter. You're both too stubborn to admit that the other person might have a valid point of view,' she continued calmly, and Linda bit back the retort she wanted to make.

'I expect you're right,' she said instead, and Wanda laughed.

'That's it, humour me because I'm a patient! But I'm not, and really I don't mind if you disagree with me. What about this young man Jamie keeps on about—tell me about him,' she invited.

Linda was thrown for a moment. 'Paul lives with me—well, no, that isn't actually the case,' she hurried on, seeing Wanda's astonished expression. 'I mean, there's nothing between us, but Jamie thinks there is, and nothing I say will make him change his mind,' she said sadly.

'If this Paul is normal, then I suppose Jamie has good reason for believing you're lovers.'

Linda found the other woman's direct gaze almost as disconcerting as she found Jamie's, and she shrugged, not wanting to discuss her private life with her. 'How will you manage when you go home? Do you live alone?' she asked instead, and Wanda seemed to accept the change of subject, for she went on to describe her country cottage, the busy life she led, the many friends she entertained. 'I'm glad to be going back—a little of Jamie goes a long way,' she added, with a sharp look.

Linda, determined not to rise to the bait, changed the subject yet again. 'Is there anything I can do to help you when you move back? I'd be happy to take some of your luggage,' she offered.

'That's sweet of you, and I may take you up on that, though I expect Jamie has everything organised. He's a very organised type of man,' Wanda went on, but Linda merely smiled. She'd had enough of Jamie Grainger and his organising for one day! Earlier, they'd had yet another disagreement over the running of the Clinic, and about the degree of involvement she ought to have with the patients, and she felt she had come off worst. As Wanda said, a little of him went a long way!

Her face clouded as she reflected how different it might have been. Despite his stubbornness, she loved Jamie, wanted him with every fibre of her being. True, their relationship would always be a stormy one, but at least life with him would never be dull! She got up to go, glad that Wanda apparently didn't feel the need to talk, but was waved down again.

'No, you mustn't go yet, Linda. Stay and have some coffee, I'd like you to,' Wanda added as Linda hesitated. 'I want to tell you about my daughter, but Jamie says we——'

Linda nearly lost her temper. 'I shouldn't worry too

much about what Jamie says, if I were you! If you feel the need to talk, then I'm happy to listen—though I don't mean to pry, of course.'

'I don't think Jamie means it quite like that, my dear. It's just that it's hard for him to speak of Chrissie himself—they were very much in love, you know,' Wanda continued, and Linda half rose.

'In love? Were they? Yes, I suppose they were,' she said, almost to herself. That explained a lot, though not everything. 'Was she very beautiful?' she hurried on, and Wanda got up and rummaged in a drawer of the elegant sideboard.

'I keep putting her photograph away. Once I'd grieved properly, Jamie thought it best. Yet sometimes I think Chrissie will walk through that door again. Silly, isn't it?' She handed Linda a small photograph in a silver frame. The face of a girl of about eighteen stared back at her. Certainly Chrissie had been pretty, though not in the conventional sense. A plump, happy face smiled out of the photograph, and one would have thought she hadn't a care in the world.

'She was lovely, Wanda. You haven't a more recent photo, I suppose?' asked Linda, and Wanda laughed shortly.

'That *was* recent. She was twenty-nine then, and the following year she was dead. She drowned while out swimming with a group of people she knew only slightly. I think they'd all had too much to drink, and none of them was in a fit state to save her. Perhaps she didn't care one way or the other,' Wanda went on thoughtfully, as she took the photograph from Linda and replaced it in the drawer, shutting it with a decisive movement.

'I'm sure she would have wanted to live, Wanda. She

looks the sort of girl who enjoyed life,' Linda assured her.

'Yes, she did, but I'm afraid a little of Chrissie went a long way, as well! I say that about Jamie, but naturally I don't mean it. He's a caring, adult human being, whereas Chrissie didn't care about anyone except Chrissie. It surprises me that he stayed married to her for so long, but being a psychiatrist I suppose he——'

'Married!' exclaimed Linda, wide-eyed. 'Chrissie was his ex-wife? I knew he'd been divorced, but I didn't connect the two facts, I'm afraid.'

'Oh, I thought you knew that? Didn't Jamie say? Typical of him. You must have known I was his mother-in-law, though—didn't you?' Wanda's glance was searching, and Linda felt a swift tide of colour suffuse her face.

'No, no, I didn't—I thought you were his girlfriend,' she admitted, and Wanda sank down on to the settee and laughed until the tears ran down her cheeks.

By the time Wanda had recovered herself, the cat had reappeared and decided to investigate Linda, who put out her hand tentatively, wishing she could slink out of the room as the cat had done earlier. She felt such a fool, but she couldn't have been expected to know about Jamie and Chrissie, nor could she have imagined that the glamorous Wanda was his mother-in-law. If no one chose to tell her, there was no reason to feel embarrassed—but if Wanda was to tell Jamie!

'There you are, my darling!' Wanda slid off the settee and enfolded the cat in her arms. 'Isn't he a pet? Rather like Jamie sometimes!' she added, her eyes still full of laughter, and this time Linda joined in.

It was, Linda reflected as she left some while later, quite a morning. Wanda's revelations meant that Jamie

was free after all—or was he? Remembering Anne
Redmond, she wasn't so sure. How he must have
laughed to himself when she had told him to keep his
kisses for Wanda! That rankled—he could at least have
referred to Wanda as his mother-in-law. No, instead he
had been laughing at her silently all the while, letting
her go on believing that he and Wanda were lovers. How
dared he!

Feeling anything but benevolent towards mankind in
general, and Jamie Grainger in particular, she decided to
call in at her cottage on the way back to the Clinic.
There was an article she wanted to photocopy, and she
needed at least a few minutes to herself before facing
Jamie once more.

If she had hoped that Paul would be out or even away
on his increasingly frequent trips, she was to be disappointed, and she hesitated about going in. She couldn't
face *anyone* at the moment, and if Paul was in a clinging
mood, she might well say something she would regret.
He beamed at her as she opened the sitting-room door.
'Didn't expect you back yet, Lindy—have they given
you a half day? That's good,' he hurried on, brandishing
a sheaf of paper at her. 'I've got two chapters for you to
type. They need——'

'For once, it's a question of what *I* need!' Linda said
smoothly. 'I haven't got the afternoon off, but even if I
had, I wouldn't want to spend it crouched over a
typewriter! I've had a dreadful morning one way and
another, so please don't badger me.'

'Sorry,' mumbled Paul, turning his back on her and
bending his head over his work again. Linda stood there
for a moment, knowing she ought to apologise but not
feeling like it. It wasn't fair to Paul and she'd had no
right to snap at him.

'Look, I'm sorry,' she said awkwardly, 'but I'm not in a very sociable mood at present. I'll cook you a special dinner to make up—all right?' Without waiting for him to comment, she stalked out, picked up the magazine, then hurried back to her car. She sat behind the wheel for a little while, eyes closed, trying desperately to relax, the way she was always telling the patients they must! Taking her own advice was far harder than handing it out, though, and she was still tense and angry when she finally arrived back at the Clinic.

Jamie was in the car park as she stopped her car, and she waved briefly, then quickened her pace. She simply wasn't in the right mood for his quicksilver wit and barbed comments, but she wasn't to escape.

He followed her, and she whirled round, prepared to do battle. His smile disarmed her, though, and they stood staring at each other for a moment. 'Not going to eat me, Sister Scott?' he asked mildly, and she shook her head.

'No, Thursday isn't my day for eating psychiatrists!' she quipped. 'It's shaping up to be one of those days— do you know that, Dr Grainger?' she asked, her head on one side, and he smiled gently down at her.

'I know the feeling,' he agreed. 'Wanda phoned, told me I had to apologise for misleading you about our relationship. She almost read the Riot Act to me,' he added, with a puzzled air.

'Knowing the situation would have spared me some embarrassment, certainly,' Linda agreed wanly. 'I was so incensed that I lashed out at poor Paul when I got home. Oh, by the way, this is the article I mentioned.' She held out the quarterly magazine, and Jamie took it, their fingers brushing for an instant. She steeled herself not to flinch, but that old chemistry or electricity was working overtime again!

'And did poor Paul retaliate?' asked Jamie, suspicion darkening his voice.

'Paul? No, he's the most mild-mannered of people. That's one point in his favour,' Linda said tightly. 'I apologised, though, and I've promised to make him a super dinner when I get home tonight so that——'

'You're coming out to dinner with me,' he said firmly, and Linda opened her mouth to protest. 'No arguments, Sister Scott—that's a direct order from your chief,' he went on.

'I cease to take orders from you at five o'clock, Doctor,' she said swiftly. 'After that, my time's my own.'

'I think you should have an evening out, enjoy some conversation, a little wine, good music, et cetera, et cetera.' That charming smile was back again, just the smile Linda most mistrusted.

'I don't know what the et cetera, et cetera, might lead to, but the answer is a resounding NO, Dr Grainger! I'm tired, I've no doubt Paul will spend the evening sulking, and I have the urge to scream—it might embarrass you if I screamed during our evening out.' She raised a brow, daring him to contradict her.

'Yes, there's something in that, I suppose. I know— I'll come to dinner with you,' he said instead. 'Just the three of us—a nice cosy little dinner for three. How about that?'

Linda wasn't sure if he was joking, but decided to take him seriously. 'I look forward to seeing you at dinner, then, Doctor. We dine about seven—please be on time,' she added officiously, and he grinned at her, before sketching a salute and sauntering away to the in-patient unit.

All of a sudden, the day took on a brighter aspect, and she turned to her next task with a return of her old enthusiasm—Jamie Grainger was coming to dinner!

As it turned out, it was dinner for two, not three, for Paul had taken himself off by the time Linda got home, leaving only a brief note to say that he had left his manuscript in his room to be typed when she had time to spare.

Linda gazed at the note in exasperation. It gave no indication where Paul had gone, or even when he would be back. He had made sure to leave her a pile to typing, though!

Promptly at seven the doorbell rang, and Linda ran downstairs, still hot and flushed from her bath. Jamie smiled at her from the doorstep, looking cool and immaculate in light cords and jacket, with a white shirt. Clasped in one large hand was a bouquet of roses, and silently he held them out to her.

With hands that trembled slightly, Linda took them. 'They're lovely, Jamie, but you shouldn't have—I'm pleased you did, though,' she added, glad to hear his husky chuckle again. Perhaps as he was a guest, he wouldn't torment her as he did at the Clinic.

A puzzled frown crossed his face as he followed her into the bright, airy sitting-room. 'Where's the great Paul, then? Not taken himself off in a fit of pique, has he?'

That remark was so near the truth that Linda couldn't deny it. 'I'm afraid you're right, but he's left me enough typing to last a month, so he'll be back.'

'Yes, they always come back,' he said testily, and a shadow crossed his face, then was quickly gone.

Unthinkingly, she put her small hand on his arm. 'I'm sorry, Jamie—about Chrissie, I mean. I—I can imagine what life would be like married to someone like Paul, and I suppose she——'

'You can't possibly imagine what marriage to Chrissie was like!' he exploded, and Linda backed off, shaken. 'She was lovely, Linda. Warm and loving, with such a sweet, gentle smile,' he went on, his eyes far away, and she stood quietly, letting him talk. At last the shadows of the past were coming out for an airing, and she knew he would feel all the better for telling her. 'And yet she could be cruel and indifferent. Sometimes it was like living with a doll—a smiling, empty-headed doll. I—I can't explain how Chrissie was—certainly she had a similar sort of personality to Winterton's. That's why I keep warning you against him, Linda.' He took her hand, startling her. 'Get rid of him, before he takes over your life and ruins it. He will if he can.'

'I know,' she breathed, afraid lest she break the spell. His touch was heating her, and for an instant she wished Paul *had* been there, to protect her from the force of her own emotions. 'But he knows there isn't any future for him with me. I imagine he's got a girlfriend some-where—some poor fool he's latched on to,' she added with a wry smile, 'since *this* poor fool has run out of patience. Anyway, sit down and make yourself at home while I see to the meal. It's only a salad, I'm afraid,' she added, already halfway to the door.

'That's fine by me, Linda. Let me help you.' To her dismay, Jamie was right behind her when she escaped to the kitchen, and, turning suddenly to open the door of the cabinet, she collided with him, his strong arms steadying her.

'Th-thank you. I'm all right now,' she said sharply,

breaking away. 'If you wouldn't mind reaching up for the Parmesan cheese—it's right at the back.'

Jamie handed her the carton of Parmesan, his smile twisted, then perched on the edge of a chair, just watching as Linda busied herself. She wished he would go, and was conscious of his gaze boring into her as she moved about the kitchen. Paul would always let her get on with her chores, respecting the fact that she didn't like anyone else in the kitchen, but she didn't think Jamie would take kindly to being ejected!

'There! All ready, Doctor. Will you do the honours and pour the wine?' she asked, trying to keep the conversation light.

Peace reigned during the prawn cocktail, and wasn't broken until they were nearly through the enormous salad. 'I'll have to get you to do the catering at the Clinic,' Jamie commented, 'this salad's delicious. Nice and crisp—none of that limp lettuce leaf and unripe tomato you get in some restaurants!'

'Thank you.' Linda was absurdly pleased at the unexpected compliment, and beamed at him. 'Do you usually eat at home? I suppose you do,' she went on, wondering whether she could find room for another slice of wholemeal bread.

'Sometimes I take people out to dinner.'

'Oh, yes! Yes, of course, I know you do,' Linda hurried on, remembering Nurse Redmond. That still rankled, though it wasn't any of her business, not really. . .

'Oh? Have you seen me out on the town recently?' Jamie put down his knife and fork and leaned towards her. Since the table was only small, that meant his face was only inches from her own, and she couldn't escape his penetrating gaze.

'No, I haven't, but Nurse Redmond said she had a date the other evening, so I let her go early and——'

'Ah, so that's it—Nurse Redmond! A lovely lady,' said Jamie, laughter in his voice, and Linda tried to keep her face expressionless.

'She's a good nurse,' she said carefully. 'Popular with the patients, as well. I find her particularly good at the relaxation classes. She——'

'I'm not asking you to give the woman a reference, Linda,' he said mildly, then leaned a little further forward and kissed the tip of her nose.

Linda sat back as if stung. There he was, wining and dining her staff nurse, then thinking he could come here and torment her! Well, it simply wasn't on. 'Would you like more bread?' she asked stiffly. 'I can easily open another loaf.'

'You're adept at changing the subject whenever we touch on a subject you don't care for. Why is that, do you suppose?' Jamie asked, leaning back in his chair and giving her that lazy smile. 'Perhaps I should analyse you?' he suggested.

'Yes, perhaps you should, Doctor. Perhaps you ought to start with yourself, though. From the first, you've done nothing except pick holes in me, criticising my private life, my relationship with Paul, letting me go on believing that you and Wanda were lovers. Then, as if that isn't enough, you take out my staff nurse—despite telling me that our professional and private lives musn't mix! You stop me from getting to know the patients better, you won't even let me invite one of them home! Now you calmly sit there——' She paused for breath, while Jamie watched with evident interest.

'Yes, Sister?' he prompted, making her madder than ever.

'You sit there and—and—' she faltered, 'tormenting me and——'

'Do I torment you, Linda? I'm sorry, I never meant to. Maybe it's myself I'm tormenting,' Jamie put in quietly, then he rose and took her in his arms. For a moment she rested her weary head against his shoulder, feeling the tears welling up behind her eyes. She wanted nothing more than to spend the rest of her life leaning on this man, sharing his burdens as well as her own, loving him, caring for him day and night. . .

Then the telephone shrilled, and, thankfully, she broke away, almost running to answer it. With any luck it would be Paul and she could keep him talking, anything to let the atmosphere cool down. She had almost blurted out that she loved Jamie, and if that ever happened, she wouldn't be able to continue at the Clinic. What a fool he would think her!

It wasn't Paul, it was a wrong number, and Linda slowly replaced the receiver. Reluctant to return to the kitchen, she wandered out into the tiny back garden, disturbing the starlings that usually hung hopefully around. Experts said birds shouldn't be fed during the spring and summer, but she was sick and tired of listening to experts, and one expert in particular! Feeling mutinous, she got some cake she had bought for Paul and scattered it around the bird-table in the centre of the small square of lawn.

'Linda?' For once, the dynamic Jamie Grainger sounded unsure of himself, and that hurt her more than anything. She turned slowly at the sound of his voice, the tears running unheeded down her face. 'Oh, Linda—don't!'

'I'm sorry, I——' she began, then ran into the open arms awaiting her. She could fight him no longer.

Jamie held her close, and she couldn't believe this was happening to her. To be in his arms, have him murmur soft words of love—it was unbelievable. Wasn't this what she had dreamed of ever since they had first met? All those silly arguments, his rules and regulations, their differing views on patient care—all these things didn't really matter any more. All that did matter was that she was in his arms, where she truly belonged.

'My poor little darling,' Jamie murmured against her hair, 'did I make you cry? I'm a brute.' He kissed away each tear as it fell, and Linda sighed happily, closing her eyes, believing she had found heaven at last. Of course the embrace didn't necessarily mean the same to Jamie as it did to her. He hadn't mentioned love, but he'd called her 'his darling' and that must mean something, surely? Paul Winterton and Wanda Hemsley faded into the background, and the sun shone brightly on the pair of them as, arm in arm, they strolled back into the cottage.

'Jamie, I——' Linda began, but he put a finger gently on her lips, preventing her from saying more. Still with his arm about her, he pulled her down on to the big leather settee by the hearth. Tenderly he kissed her closed eyelids, and she felt a trail of soft, gentle kisses land on her nose, the corner of her mouth, her throat. . . This was bliss, and she began to wonder if it could really be true. So little that was good had happened to her recently, she'd had too few rainbows in her life, and it was incredible that the man she loved might love her in return. Or was it merely 'want' rather than love? Did Jamie not share her dream of love? A shadow crossed her face, and Jamie was quick to notice.

'Linda? What is it? Tell me,' he demanded, and her eyes flicked open. His gaze was tender, his eyes loving, and she smiled tremulously. She had been a fool to doubt him—of course he loved her. Perhaps he didn't realise it yet, though!

'I was just thinking,' she began, 'about——'

'About Paul Winterton, I suppose,' he said grimly, his mood changing in an instant, and Linda felt chilled.

'No, not about him!' she protested. 'I was just thinking how much I'm enjoying your company,' she amended quickly. Now was no time to confess to her hidden love for him. 'I—perhaps I should make the coffee now?' she suggested, trying to struggle free, but to no avail.

'Making love might be better than making coffee— what do you think, Sister Scott?' Jamie asked, his good humour restored, and Linda froze. Yet wasn't that what she wanted? Say yes, her heart demanded, say no, her brain advised, and she wanted to scream. Of course she wanted to make love with Jamie—wasn't he the only man she had ever cared about? Yet. . .

'Linda?' Jamie's arms tightened about her, his hands beginning a slow, gentle caressing, and she trembled, her whole being crying out for him to continue, to take her and make her his own. A moan broke from her as he began to stroke her breast, his lips following his hand. The blouse she wore was thin and silky, and his hands were tormenting her. She felt her urgency grow to match his, and her lips parted involuntarily as his searching mouth found hers again.

Their kiss rocked the world. The heavens might not have moved, but Linda was prepared to swear that they did. Her heart and mind were filled with a vision of Jamie, he was her whole world, and if an earthquake had struck then, she wouldn't have noticed. Nothing mattered except this man and the love she felt for him.

It was Jamie who ended the embrace, just when she

had almost passed the point of no return. Linda felt
bereft as he eased his body from hers, setting her down
gently on the rug. 'I'm sorry, Linda, I never meant this
to happen.' He sounded distraught, but that was nothing
to how she felt. She had offered her all and been rejected,
held at bay because she fell far short of what Jamie
Grainger required in a woman! How could he!

'Sorry?' she echoed hollowly. 'Are you? I'm rather
sorry too.' Slowly she got to her feet, adjusting her skirt,
her face flaming. She felt physically sick, ashamed of
herself for offering to Jamie what she had offered to no
man before. When she forced herself to look at him, her
feelings must have shown, for that closed expression
crossed his handsome face again, and she had no idea
what he was thinking. But then she rarely did. Jamie
kept his own counsel, and she doubted if even Wanda
could penetrate the hidden world of his mind. Perhaps
only Chrissie had been able to do that.

'It's Chrissie, isn't it?' she whispered, light suddenly
dawning. Even from beyond the grave, Chrissie still held
sway over him. He still loved her, despite her love for no
one but herself.

He sighed. 'I apologise, Linda. I had no right.
Chrissie—she——' He hesitated, but Linda didn't want
to hear about his ex-wife. It seemed he couldn't live
without her. Even Anne Redmond must be only a
passing fancy. Only once had he given his heart and he
wasn't about to do so again.

'I understand,' she said stiffly, believing she did. At
last she knew what made him the man he was. The
tragedy of her father's life had left her mother wary of
men, and Jamie's experience with Chrissie had left him
wary of women. Jamie could never love again, and it was

her tragedy that she had fallen for the one man she could never have.

'I'd better go.' He sounded as miserable as she felt, but she hardened her heart. What he was suffering was nothing compared with her own heartache.

'Yes, perhaps you should,' she agreed. 'Paul might ring later.'

'You told me you didn't know where he was!' Jamie charged, and Linda squirmed under his direct gaze.

'I don't, but that won't stop him ringing. *He* knows where *I* am, after all. If he does ring, it will be only to ask about his manuscript, I expect,' she went on offhandedly. 'Like you, Paul thinks only of himself! I doubt if either of you has the capacity to love another human being. I'm grateful to you for stopping at the eleventh hour—otherwise we might both have regretted it. Goodnight, Jamie,' she finished curtly, and he rose, staring at her for a long moment.

Oh, how she wanted to fling herself into his arms, tell him she didn't mean it, that whatever Chrissie had done to him, she understood. She would love him enough for both of them, show him what true love really was. But she could say none of those things, and it was a cold-eyed stranger who left the cottage, not looking back as he made for his car.

Linda watched from the window, her heart winging its way after him as he drove off. Without Jamie, her life was empty, her future a dull greyish-blue. Depressed patients often described their depression as an endless blue mood, and she knew just what they meant.

CHAPTER TEN

'IT's more impressive than I'd thought, Sister,' Miss Anstey commented, as the group paused in their long walk up towards Arundel Castle.

'Yes, it is,' Linda agreed. 'It's been much restored, that's the only thing.'

It was a beautiful day, warm, with a little breeze cooling them as they walked. Linda had brought several of the day patients out to see the Castle, as she had promised. She had hired a minibus and driver for the day, and already they had enjoyed a brief scenic tour of the Arun Valley, and driven through some of the picturesque villages in the west of the county. The high point of their day out was to be the Castle, though, and she couldn't help wishing Jamie could be there with them.

She found the Barons' Hall impressive, even though it was Victorian and not the original medieval hall. Briefly she closed her eyes, trying to conjure up a sense of the past, then felt a tug at her sleeve and started guiltily. For a few moments she had forgotten her brood! 'I'm sorry, I——' she began, then heard the patients' quiet laughter as Jamie Grainger smiled at her.

'Oh! What are you doing here?' she hurried on, knowing she sounded ungracious but caught off guard and not knowing quite *what* to say. After that evening at her home, Jamie had seemed to be avoiding her.

'Not much of a welcome, is it, ladies?' Jamie half turned to the smiling patients. 'Never mind, since I *am* here, shall we continue the tour?' he suggested, and Linda nodded unhappily.

'Yes, naturally, Doctor.' Her tone was cordial but no more, and she was aware of his sharp gaze as he shepherded the little flock out of the hall and along to the next room.

The Picture Gallery was astonishing, at least Linda found it so, and she and Miss Anstey lingered there rather longer than they should have done. The Gallery stretched unendingly, its walls hung with portraits of the Dukes and Duchesses of Norfolk, and by her side, Miss Anstey sighed. 'They all look so rich and important, don't they?' she commented, 'but not really happy.'

Linda glanced sharply at her. 'Even the happiest of people have their off days, Miss Anstey. I've got a useful, fulfilling job, but sometimes I feel like screaming when everything goes wrong!' she added lightly, and Miss Anstey snorted, clearly not believing her.

By the time they reached the Armoury, a room full of grim reminders of ancient warfare, Linda's head was spinning. So much magnificence in one short visit gave her mental indigestion, and she was as eager as the patients to browse through the gift shop. As she counted heads, she became aware that she had lost one, but even as she set out to search, Jamie hove into view with Mrs Ellershaw who had, she informed Linda, been quite taken with the case of huge stuffed owls!

Linda was vividly aware of Jamie's presence. After restoring Mrs Ellershaw to her, he moved away and began chatting to one of the Castle staff. Then he strolled back to the patients, sharing a smile here, a word there, the ladies hanging on to his every word. One of them was nearly seventy, but that didn't stop her responding to a handsome man smiling at her, and Linda's heart warmed to him. Despite his faults, he genuinely cared for his patients, even if he patently didn't care for Sister Linda Scott!

The Castle souvenir shop kept the patients busy, and Linda found herself standing beside Jamie a few minutes later, as he ran a practised eye over the merchandise displayed. There was a group of French schoolchildren eagerly darting from one souvenir to the next, most of them buying the sticks of rock, she noticed. Uneasily aware that she ought to say something to Jamie, but not knowing what, she drifted away and went in search of a gift for her mother, finally deciding on a little green Wedgwood dish.

'That's very pretty,' Jamie commented softly, and, flushed, she whirled round.

'Yes, isn't it! I thought I'd take it home to Mum, she likes that sort of thing.'

Their seventy-year-old had also bought one of the little pottery dishes, but most had settled for tea-towels and small items marked with the name of the Castle. Mrs Ellershaw came up, brandishing two sticks of Arundel Castle rock and insisting upon giving Linda one. 'Here you are, love—it isn't much, but I don't suppose I'm allowed to buy you anything else!'

Touched, Linda accepted the rock, thinking as she did so that Jamie had been right about Mrs Ellershaw finding her own friends. She had become friends with a lady who had been quite severely depressed and they looked after each other at day patients.

Jamie was the last to leave the shop, and they waited for him outside, Linda glanced at her group, mentally assessing how the day had gone for them. Most were chatting away as though they had known one another for years, only Miss Anstey stood a little aloof.

Linda went across to her. 'Have you enjoyed yourself? I know we're a bit like day-trippers off to the whelk stalls, but it hasn't been too bad, has it?' Since Miss Anstey had always maintained that she was different from the others, Linda had been in two minds about asking her, and hadn't exerted any persuasion. To her surprise, the woman had seemed keen on coming, but now she frowned.

'No, it hasn't been too bad, I suppose,' she acknowledged. 'I thought I ought to come, force myself to mix with the others, get out of myself a bit, but I don't think it's been a great success. Oh, I've enjoyed seeing over the Castle, even bought a few souvenirs, but——' She sighed, seemingly unable to go on.

Linda put a hand on her arm, making Miss Anstey meet her gaze. 'You don't really like the others, do you? They're perhaps not your type of people?' she suggested, and Miss Anstey reddened. 'There's no need to be ashamed of the feeling. We can't all like the same things, the same pleasures, even the same people. That's what makes our work so interesting, you know—people *are* different. Would you enjoy a visit to the theatre, perhaps? We might arrange something once the season starts,' Linda suggested, and Miss Anstey brightened visibly.

Satisfied that she had done something useful for at least one of the patients, Linda glanced about for Jamie, who seemed to be a long time in the shop. She couldn't imagine him souvenir-hunting, but then what did she know of him? And naturally he would want to choose something for Wanda. As promised, she had telephoned Wanda to let her know which day they were coming into West Sussex, and they were all invited back for late tea.

Jamie had received the news without comment, but Linda presumed he wouldn't be coming.

She forced a smile as he approached, two paper bags clasped firmly. 'I've left my car in the Castle car park, Sister, I'll follow you to Wanda's. Must put these away first.' He seemed in a good mood, and Linda relaxed slightly. At least he wasn't going to take her to task for accepting Wanda's invitation!

'Oh, by the way——' He turned back as if a thought had just struck him, and her tenseness returned. Now what?

'Yes, Doctor?' she said calmly, feeling anything but.

'Your friend Richard the Third—*he* has some connection with Arundel—did you know that? I bought you a guidebook.' Jamie rummaged in one of his bags and produced the illustrated guide, his smile wary as he handed it over.

Taken aback, Linda said, 'Thank you, I'll read it on the way back. Did he stay here, then?'

'I don't think so, but one of the Howard family was a friend of his. He was killed at Bosworth Field, apparently. Richard created him first Duke of Norfolk. He may have helped finish off the Princes in the Tower!' he added, with a wicked grin. 'I'll catch you up later!'

Wanda was waiting for them as the minibus parked in front of her cottage. It was small, much smaller than Jamie's home, and surrounded by a garden glorious with summer blooms. Linda heard the patients murmur appreciatively as they got out to stretch their legs.

'Your garden's lovely,' Linda told her. 'It's a joy to sit out here, I should imagine.'

'Some of the shrubs in the Clinic grounds came out of my garden, you know. Jamie chose the ones he wanted,' Wanda commented, smiling a welcome at them all.

'Come in, ladies, make yourselves at home! My cat has taken himself off for the day, I'm afraid, but—ah, Jamie!' Wanda waved energetically as Jamie's car appeared in the narrow, winding lane, and Linda watched wistfully as he pecked his mother-in-law on the cheek.

Fluffy was nowhere in evidence, but there was a blue budgie in a big cage in a corner of the spacious sitting-room, and Linda went over to talk to it, feeling somehow deflated. She had enjoyed her day with the others, but seeing Jamie had awakened all the old longing, and she felt vaguely dissatisfied, as if the day ought to have given her more and had not. 'Pretty boy, pretty boy, who's a pretty boy, then?' she said to the bird, who put its head on one side, as if trying to sum her up.

'I hope that's me you're talking about!' a familiar voice teased, and, astonished, Linda whirled around—to find Paul beaming at her.

'What are you doing here?' she gasped. 'I thought you'd gone back to your sister?'

Paul shrugged, and looked uncomfortable. 'Well, I did, but she threw me out, and then I met Wanda—well, that was accidental, but she's obviously got a kind heart, so she invited me to stay.' Paul was about to say more, then Linda saw who was hovering behind him.

'May I ask what you're doing here, Mr Winterton?' Jamie's voice was calm, reasoned, the sort of voice he used for difficult patients, and Paul seemed taken aback.

'Well, you know how it is, Doc. Linda said——'

'I'll speak to Sister later,' Jamie went on smoothly, 'but my mother-in-law didn't mention that she had a guest.' He waited, but it looked as though Paul wasn't going to answer him, then Wanda appeared.

'Isn't that wonderful! Paul knew one of Chrissie's

friends! They were at school together. It was quite by chance I met him—you remember Nick?' She turned to Jamie, her face alight, and Linda watched the tableau, belonging yet not belonging. This was a matter for Jamie and Wanda to sort out between them, but she *had* brought Paul into the area and any blame for his appearance here must rest partly with her.

Jamie nodded grimly, and Wanda hurried on, her smile embracing all of them, 'Well, Paul was spending the night at Nick's, and we got talking and—well, here we are! It's lovely to have some young company again,' she enthused, then her eyes narrowed as she noticed Jamie's lack of enthusiasm.

'Yes, I imagine it is,' was his comment. 'It must be rather like having Chrissie home again!' The meaning of his words wasn't lost on Linda, and Paul, meanwhile, had disappeared. Linda set off in search of him. Even if it was the only thing she ever did for Wanda, she must get rid of Paul.

She found him chatting easily to the patients, and had to wait until he finished charming Miss Anstey—or trying to, for that lady wasn't easily fooled. 'Paul, have you a minute? I wanted to ask you about the manuscript,' she said, taking him firmly by the arm and leading him away.

'Good lord, yes!' He clapped a hand to his head in a comical gesture. 'Do you know, so much has happened, I'd almost forgotten the typing! Have you finished it yet?'

'I haven't had time to even begin,' Linda said grimly. 'I *do* have my living to earn as well. Why don't you get an agency to type it for you? Anyway, what are you doing here? Dr Grainger's furious!' That was the understatement of the year. Though he didn't show it, Jamie was building up to explode, rather like a volcano that erupts and amazes everyone who had lived in its shadow for years. He wouldn't take out his temper on Paul, but Linda had no doubt *she* would feel the sharp edge of his tongue. Well, she wasn't going to put up with it!

'I don't see why he should be,' mumbled Paul, then brightened as their hostess approached. 'Linda was just saying I shouldn't be here, Wanda—I'm sorry, I didn't realise I was a nuisance.'

Wanda's face clouded. 'Of course you aren't! I'm sure Linda never intended to say such a thing! Did you?' She turned her sweet smile on Linda, who shifted uneasily. Trust Paul to put her on the spot.

'Paul *can* be a nuisance,' she said firmly, aware of his astonished expression. 'Dr Grainger doesn't want you to be burdened with a guest at the moment, Wanda, and perhaps it would be better if Paul came back to my cottage.' That was the last thing she wanted, but it was better than having him take over Wanda's life.

'That's very sweet of you, my pet, but I'm really quite comfortable here.' Paul turned his charming smile on Wanda, even though he spoke to Linda. 'Wanda says I can stay for a few days—I promise not to stay longer,' he added silkily.

'Your——' Linda began, then stopped. She had been about to say that his few days had a habit of becoming months, but now wasn't the time. It wasn't fair to Wanda, who was looking decidedly unhappy at this turn of events. She was so sweet, so trusting, that Linda's heart ached for her. Having a daughter like Chrissie ought to have warned Wanda, but clearly it hadn't—or perhaps in some strange way, Paul was a substitute for her daughter. She might have seen more of Chrissie in him than she was prepared to admit.

Jamie was the only one who could sort out this mess, but he was nowhere in sight, and when she glanced out of the window, Linda saw that his car had gone. It was unlike him to abandon people in their hour of need, but that was exactly what he had done, and she felt bereft.

The patients enjoyed their tea, and Linda made an effort for their sakes. Paul was in good form, laughing and joking with them, so that made it easier. If he harboured any resentment against her for saying he could be a nuisance, he hid it well, and she gave him full marks for that. When he wanted, he could be very pleasant, and perhaps she had overreacted. Surely Wanda could cope with him? Once his book found a publisher, he might return to London, or to the girlfriend she was convinced he had hidden away somewhere. There were endless possibilities, and she decided she was worrying over nothing. At least *she* was free of him for a while!

Pleased, she gave Paul a warm smile when he asked her something, and he looked taken aback for a moment before that smug, arrogant expression crept back. She tried to ignore it—remember, she told herself, the quicker you type his wretched book, the sooner you'll be rid of him!

On the way back, the ladies chatted among themselves, only Miss Anstey and Linda herself remaining silent. Once or twice one of them spoke to her, and Linda replied, showed interest in souvenirs, but her mind was far away, on a man who had deserted her when she needed his comfort and advice. That was something for which she couldn't forgive him.

Jamie was interviewing when Linda finally returned to the Clinic. Officially she was off duty now, but she was determined to speak to him, no matter how long she had to stay.

Her head was bent over the staff roster when he at length appeared, and she caught a whiff of his expensive after-shave before she finally glanced up, acknowledging his presence with a cool smile.

'Busy, Sister?' he asked, unknotting his tie and rolling it up, Linda's eyes involuntarily following the movement.

'I'm always busy, Dr Grainger,' she said smoothly. 'Which patient were you interviewing? Is she someone for the day unit?' At least they were on safe ground when discussing patients!

'It was a he, and no, he isn't for day patients. I might need to admit him later.' Jamie leant against the door, hands in pockets, pale eyes watchful, and Linda began to feel uncomfortable. 'Arundel Castle,' he murmured. 'Did they enjoy it? We must book up other day trips for the ladies if that one was a success—was it?'

Linda nodded. 'Everyone had a good day, I think, except Miss Anstey. It wasn't really her choice of a day out, so I suggested a theatre visit and she perked up. Maybe we could——'

Jamie's chuckle stopped her. 'Still planning, Linda? I'm glad we employed you—you're like a breath of fresh air to this place,' he said, startling her.

'Thank you—I think,' she said slowly, her blue eyes puzzled.

He came further into the room, staring down at his tie for a moment. 'I'm sorry I couldn't stay at Wanda's, but——'

'That's all right. Really, I understand. I didn't know you had an interview, and you're lecturing tonight, aren't you?' All of a sudden, Linda's ire vanished and she forgot that she was supposed to take him to task for abandoning her. I'm sorry about Paul—about him lodging with Wanda, I mean,' she hurried on. 'Is there any danger in it, do you think? He'll leave once his book is finished,' she added slowly, and Jamie grimaced.

'He's gone already—I popped back and chucked him out once the patients left.' He stared at her, his expression defying her to challenge his right to do that.

'You told Paul to go?' Linda couldn't believe her ears.

He reddened under her scrutiny, and she watched with interest as a slow tide of colour swept up from his neck to his face. 'I didn't actually *tell* him, no,' he admitted reluctantly. 'I showed him the door and offered to carry his luggage out. He got the idea, I believe,' he went on grimly.

Linda's lips quivered, but she tried desperately not to laugh. 'I wish I'd been there!' Then her amusement faded as she visualised Paul moving back in with her. 'I wonder where he's gone now?'

'Not back to the cottage, I can assure you of that. I suggested a return to London and he agreed meekly. That's the way he was heading when he left, anyway.' Jamie rubbed the side of his face reflectively. 'I called in at your cottage afterwards and peered through the window, but there was no sign of him, and his car wasn't there.'

'Oh, good. He's still got a few items of clothing there, though, and his precious manuscript—he won't go far without *that*,' she emphasised.

'When he comes back, give me a ring, Linda, and I'll sort him out,' he offered.

'That's kind of you, but it might make matters worse. I usually do my *own* sorting out,' Linda said succinctly. 'I'm a bit of a bossy Bessie at times, and I can handle Paul,' she assured him.

Jamie seemed amused. 'That's splendid,' he said, then glanced at his watch. 'I'd better get ready for my lecture, I suppose.' He hesitated a fraction before saying. 'I was thinking about an early dinner—you haven't time to join me, I suppose?'

A surprised Linda said yes without giving herself time to consider if it was wise, and Jamie's face lit up. Of course, later, she realised that it most certainly *wasn't* wise, but she had no intention of backing out now.

She smiled at her reflection in her dressing-table mirror, pleased because her new dress exactly matched the colour of her eyes. If anything, the dress accentuated their clear blue, and she decided she needed only a touch of gold mascara to colour her pale lashes.

Hurriedly dabbling on a little of her favourite perfume, she was ready with time to spare, then spent the next few minutes wondering what—if anything—to read into Jamie's invitation. It was simply a hurried meal with a colleague, she realised. He was lonely and didn't want to eat alone, so he had invited her to join him simply because she was the only one left in the unit. That must be the only reason, mustn't it? Her traitorous heart wanted to believe otherwise, but that way lay heartbreak.

Dinner was a hurried affair, but for once they sat in a companionable silence, Linda making only monsyllabic replies to Jamie's few remarks as they neared the end of the meal.

'Cheese omelette and salad isn't the most glamorous of dishes, but I promise to take you somewhere more exotic next time,' he told her, as they sipped their coffee.

That sounded good, and Linda smiled over at him, thinking how wonderful it would be if they could dine together every evening, spend every night in one house, in one bed, spend the rest of their lives in each other's arms. . . 'I enjoy omelettes,' she said instead, the glorious dream fading and workaday realities intruding once more. She had no idea who *did* spend time in Jamie's bed, but it was unlikely he was entirely celibate—he was far too male for that!

'Shall we go? I don't want to hurry you, but——' Jamie indicated the clock, and Linda obediently rose. It was good of him to take her to dinner, and she wondered wistfully if it meant he really *was* free. Perhaps Anne Redmond was just a passing fancy and he had grown tired of her already. There was always hope.

'Aren't you on holiday next week?' Jame took her arm as they walked to the car park. 'I had a note of it, but our Nursing Officer's been filing things again and I think he's filed papers I hadn't finished with!'

'It wasn't supposed to be until the end of August, but he asked me to bring it forward. It doesn't matter to me when I go, actually,' Linda confessed. 'I'm only going home, and Mum doesn't mind when I turn up.'

'That's good,' he said slowly, his touch burning her as he still kept hold of her arm. 'I'll drop you back at the Clinic so you can pick up your car, unless you'd like to go straight back to the cottage and get a taxi in tomorrow?' he suggested.

'I can walk to the Clinic from here, Jamie—you go home and get ready for your lecture. I'm fine, really,' she assured him, noting the air of strain that was beginning to show again. To think that once she had thought him unfeeling, untouched by human emotions!

He smiled into her eyes. 'It's no trouble—but might I ask you a favour?'

Glad she could do something for him, Linda smiled. 'Ask away!'

'I suggest you take your holiday earlier now it's been

re-scheduled. And——' He hesitated, and she wondered what was coming next. She couldn't take any more surprises for one day. 'My car's going to be off the road for a day or two and I'd like to beg a lift to Stratford. I've a few days owing to me and I promised an old friend I'd pop in to see her at the weekend. She's looking forward to seeing me and I don't want to disappoint her,' he went on with a faint smile, and Linda tried hard to ignore the green-eyed monster that was lurking behind her. 'If you could drop me in the town, you wouldn't be burdened with my company on the way back—I can easily get a train home,' he added, seeing her hesitation.

'Oh, no, you wouldn't be a burden!' she assured him. Far from it! 'I needn't stay for a whole week; Mum might come back with me now that Paul's gone—if he *has* gone,' she amended.

'Fine,' Jamie said easily. 'I'll look forward to a very pleasant weekend,' he added, still with that little smile, and Linda tried hard to be pleased for him, but somehow couldn't manage it. The 'old friend' probably wasn't the glamorous girlfriend she had envisaged, but who could say?

'He's taller than you said he was,' Mrs Scott commented, as Linda helped her mother lay the table for lunch. 'Handsomer too.'

'Now, Mum, stop matchmaking!' laughed Linda. 'He's heavily committed and I'm simply not interested, so please leave it.' If her mother knew that was a lie, she didn't say so, and she hoped the message had sunk in: Dr Grainger was merely a friend and a colleague, no more than that. There was definitely *no* romance in their relationship!

Jamie had, predictably, charmed her mother, and

although Linda didn't know how it had happened she found that they were putting him up for the final night of his stay. 'You'd think he'd want to stay with his friend, wouldn't you?' Linda said as she watched Jamie washing her car—a chore he had willingly taken on.

'You would think so, yes,' her mother agreed. 'Was it much bother driving him up here? Not one of these back seat drivers, is he? Thinks the weak little woman can't do anything as well as a man,' Mrs Scott went on acidly.

'No, he didn't try to drive for me. In fact, he fell asleep once we were past London! He said I was a restful driver, and that it surprised him since I was such a fiery person!'

Mother and daughter were still chuckling over that as Jamie appeared at the back door, in old checked shirt and jeans, wiping his grimy hands on an old rag. 'Was that a joke I can share? Or was it strictly girl-talk?' he asked, sniffing appreciatively. 'Is that my lunch—can I have a preview?'

'Questions, questions—you wait and see, young man,' Mrs Scott said firmly, before bustling out, leaving Linda not knowing quite what to say to him, beyond thanking him for washing her car.

'Thank you for washing Esmeralda,' she said stiltedly, and Jamie pulled his forelock.

'Anything for the little miss,' he said amicably. 'Are you sure I can't have a preview of the lunch? It smells appetising.'

'Mum's meals always do, and no, you can't, so——' The telephone began its soft purring, and Linda sighed.

'I hope that isn't another of Mum's friends. They keep popping up all over the place!' She'd known how popular her mother was, and how many friends and acquaintances she had, but they seemed to have increased tenfold in the last few months!—another reason for her mother's refusing to move down to Sussex and to share her cottage.

It wasn't a friend of her mother's, far from it, it was Paul Winterton, and Linda lowered her voice, hoping Jamie wouldn't realise who the caller was. 'Yes? Can I help you?'

'Ah—is the great man there, by any chance?' Paul whispered back. 'It sounds as though he is! I've nearly finished the last chapter, but I haven't been feeling too grand——' He broke off as a fit of coughing overtook him, and Linda's eyes widened. Paul wasn't the healthiest of individuals, but the middle of a warm spell wasn't likely to do him any harm. 'Could I come back, Lindy? Just to finish the book? Then you'll be rid of me—for ever, probably,' he went on gloomily, and Linda glared at the phone. That was typical of him!

'I doubt that you're dying, Paul,' she said, abandoning all pretence that the caller was one of her mother's friends. 'Yes, I've finished typing the two chapters you left me and I've done all the corrections, and no, you *can't* come back!'

There was a silence at the other end, but Linda hardened her heart against Paul's blandishments. To her surprise, he seemed to accept the inevitable. 'All right, Lindy, I know when I'm not wanted. I'll leave the last chapter in your outhouse, shall I? When will you be back?'

'On Tuesday, I expect. Come to see and we can sort out any problems with the final chapter. I'll see you then.' Linda replaced the receiver, her thoughts troubled. If she didn't let Paul stay, he might just return to Wanda, and *she* wasn't likely to send him on his way. Wanda was already at loggerheads with Jamie over the abrupt way he had sent Paul packing, and would probably be only too delighted to have him back again.

Jamie hadn't moved from the spot, and Linda's expression was wary as she met his reproving gaze. 'I know, I know, I shouldn't let him even inside the door, but I *did* promise to finish his book. I owe him that,' she said simply, and Jamie's gaze sharpened.

'Unless you've been lovers, I wouldn't have thought you owed him anything,' he said levelly. 'But it isn't any of my business, is it?' He gazed down at the rag he was holding. 'I'll finish the car, then I hope to sample that delicious meal—whatever it is!' he finished lightly, and Linda watched him go, a lump in her throat. He still believed she and Paul had shared more than a home, and she was in no mood to tell him otherwise. As he said, it wasn't his business, and wishing it was wouldn't solve any of her problems!

'It seems strange being back in Sussex,' Linda commented, as they passed through Uckfield early the next morning. She cast a sideways glance at Jamie, who appeared half asleep by her side. 'Did you enjoy your long weekend with your friend?' If he had, then of course she would be delighted for him, but. . .

'Mm, very much so. We sat up half the night talking over old times.' There was a satisfied smile on Jamie's face.

'Oh, good, I'm glad.' Linda tried to inject some warmth into her voice. 'At last, a nice straight run home!'

'Do you think of Sussex as home now? That's good.'

She considered. 'To be honest, nowhere is *really* home. I'm a bit of a gypsy, I suppose. I left home early, even before I started my training—London was my goal then.

The bright lights palled after a while, though. Then Gran died and left me the cottage, and when I saw the post at the Summerheath advertised, it seemed like the answer to a prayer!'

'Or a dream?' Jamie suggested.

'Yes, perhaps it was,' she agreed quietly. That he had become part of that dream was something he would never know.

She offered to drop him at his own home, but he insisted on returning with her first. 'Just to see that everything's all right,' he said firmly, and she knew he meant Paul. To be honest, she was glad he was coming back with her. She hated going back to an empty cottage after a trip away, and without Jamie it seemed lonely, even though the neighbour she had taken to hospital popped in from time to time. She was at her window when Linda drew up outside the cottages, and Jamie commented on it.

'I saw at least *one* net curtain twitch! You'll be getting talked about.'

'I expect they're glad to see me back! You know how neighbours are if they know you're a nurse—or a doctor, I suppose—they're eager to tell you their symptoms or show you their operation scars, or——'

'Or tell you how many hours they spent in childbirth with each of their children,' Jamie finished for her, getting out of the small car and stretching his legs. 'Give me your key and I'll look around for you—see to your welcoming committee,' he went on, nodding towards Mrs Honeysett, who came out of her cottage, waving.

'You've got a visitor, Sister—I've called the doctor, but he hasn't come yet! Should we get an ambulance, do you think? Still, your Dr Grainger's here now, isn't he!' She beamed at Jamie.

'What exactly is the matter with Sister's visitor?' Jamie asked gently, but Linda didn't wait to hear. Still clutching the key, she ran to her cottage. It must be Paul! It couldn't be anyone else, but how had he got in? He'd had a key once, but after he left she had changed the locks, determined that if he turned up unexpectedly, he would have to wait until she let him in.

All sorts of alarming thoughts rushed through her mind as she fumbled with the front door key, then hurried from room to room, seeking the 'visitor' Mrs Honeysett had spoken of, but the cottage was empty, and clearly no one had broken in.

It was Jamie who found him, and when she came downstairs again, there was Jamie carrying in the recumbent figure of Paul—a dirty, unshaven and unkempt Paul whose bloodshot eyes opened slightly, and whose cracked lips tried to smile at her.

'Hello, Lindy,' he croaked. 'I couldn't get in and I felt too poorly to force a window, so I slept in the outhouse. Ah, thank you, Doctor, that's lovely.'

Linda watched as Jamie laid him on the settee. Since Paul wasn't a tall man, the settee fitted him perfectly, and Jamie gently drew a cover over him, before turning to her. 'I don't think we need worry too much—he's none the worse for sleeping in your outhouse for the past night or so.' With what Linda considered callous indifference, he dismissed Paul's plight.

'Thank you, Dr Grainger,' she said formally. 'I'll see to him now—or shall I drive you home first?'

'I'm in no hurry to get back,' Jamie retorted, clearly stung by her icy tone. 'I'll see to the patient—if you get him something soothing to drink it will ease his throat a bit.' He continued to stare down at the silent Paul, and Linda wondered what he was thinking.

She left them, and heard Jamie's heavy tread on the stairs a couple of times. When she returned to the sitting-room, Paul was sitting in the armchair, freshly bathed and looking remarkably spruce.

Paul accepted the cool drink gratefully, his eyes on Linda as he drank, while Jamie stood as if on guard. She resented that, but could say nothing while Paul was within earshot. 'I've suggested to Winterton that he spends the night at the General—they'll find a bed for him. I think twenty-four hours' observation should be sufficient,' Jamie went on, and Paul nodded obediently, the way Linda often found herself doing whenever Jamie issued orders!

'Yes, of course, Doctor. Whatever you say,' Paul murmured, then smiled at Linda, though his dark eyes remained sad. 'I expect Lindy will be glad of her home to herself again—won't you?' His tone was wistful and Linda was about to invite him to stay for a while, but something in Jamie's stance warned her that he wouldn't stand for that, and he was right, anyway. It simply wouldn't do.

'I think Dr Grainger's right, Paul, a night under hospital supervision will be best. Where have you been staying, anyway?' she asked, curiosity getting the better of her at last, but Paul lapsed into one of his sulky moods and refused to answer any questions.

Jamie went to ring the hospital, and she followed him, determined to have her say, no matter what. 'That isn't a particularly caring attitude you have towards Paul's illness!' she said quietly, longing to shout but refraining. 'The man's ill! Can't you see that? I know he's a pain, but the least I can do is give him a few days' respite here. He——'

'No! That's an order, Sister Scott—do I have to put it

in writing?' Jamie was coldly angry, but she wasn't about
to back down. He had too much of his own way, and
this was a private matter, nothing to do with the Clinic
at all.

'Paul is my friend,' she said stubbornly. 'If I want to
let him stay for a little while, surely that's *my* affair? I
can't see where you come into it, quite frankly,' she
hurried on, before he could blind her with logic.

'No, perhaps you can't, and if you're determined to
let him stay, I can't stop you,' he said quietly, busily
dialling. 'But as a doctor I have to insist he stays at the
General overnight—you can't argue with *that*, Sister
Scott!'

Defeated, Linda wandered back into the sitting-room,
to find a wan Paul, eyes closed, stretched out on the
settee once more. 'Oh, Lindy, send him away! I really
don't feel like spending the night at his wretched hospital,' he begged. 'I'll be all right here, honestly. I won't
be any bother.'

'Doctor's right, you need medical supervision,' Linda
said in a voice that brooked no argument. 'After the
twenty-four hours is up, we'll see.' She disliked turning
him out, but knew in her heart that Jamie was right.
Her only worry was that Wanda would take him in
afterwards, and she hoped Jamie had contingency plans
for that.

Despondently she watched as Paul was driven away in
the ambulance. Jamie went with him, and she was
without his company for the first time in nearly forty-
eight hours. It was funny, but it was Jamie she missed,
not Paul, despite the fact that Paul needed her more.

And it was Jamie she dreamt about as, after several
hours of restless tossing and turning, she at last fell
asleep.

CHAPTER ELEVEN

'HOW HAVE you been getting on at work, Mr Staplehurst?' Linda asked, and the patient stared down at his hands for a moment, clearly finding it difficult to talk about it.

'The firm have been very good,' he acknowledged gruffly, 'but you can imagine how I feel—having to admit that I've a mental illness and need to come to a place like this?' He waved a hand to indicate the Clinic. 'No, of course you can't imagine it,' he went on, with a gusty sigh. 'No one can, if they haven't experienced it for themselves.'

'That isn't quite true,' Linda said firmly. 'I've never been a patient at the Clinic or anywhere like it, but that doesn't mean I can't sympathise with you. Your wife knows your problem as well—does she offer support?' Sometimes the burden of support fell on the spouse, and often it was too much.

'She doesn't understand why an intelligent grown man should have this compulsion to go around checking every window at least ten times before he leaves for work in the morning, hurry home at lunchtime to do the very same thing, then go through the whole rigmarole again in the evening. Would *you* understand it, Sister?' Mr Staplehurst looked defiant, and there was no stock answer Linda could give him.

'If I weren't a nurse then, no, I suppose I might not, but your wife does. Dr Grainger spoke to her yesterday,' Linda said gently. 'She may not know *why* you do it or how to cure you, but she understands the anxiety that's raging away inside you, and she'd like to help.'

'Raging anxiety? Yes, that's a good way of describing it,' the patient said thoughtfully. 'That's what it is—a compulsion to follow a set pattern of behaviour, just to ease that raging anxiety.'

'But it doesn't, does it? At least, not for long,' Linda pointed out. 'Dr Grainger will be back shortly, and he can explain it better than I can. I'm afraid he's over-worked and underpaid, like most NHS doctors. Psychiatrists, even consultant ones, aren't any different!' Often their patients didn't want to think there was anyone else in the entire world who suffered as much as they did, but Linda felt Mr Staplehurst came into a different category. Stressing that even psychiatrists had problems, including overwork, might touch off some sympathetic response in the man, and she was proved right. They were busily discussing ways of reorganising the Health Service when Jamie at last appeared, his hair damp and slightly curling from the heavy shower of rain.

'I see Sister's been keeping you busy,' he observed, his eyes kindly as they rested on the patient. 'Don't let her boss you around—I have to keep her in line!'

Mr Staplehurst gave the first laugh Linda had heard from him, and she left him to Jamie's care, closing the door softly behind her. If only Jamie could always be so pleasant! Just lately he had become unbearable.

No, unbearable wasn't the right word, she conceded, trying to be fair to him. Just unapproachable, at least to her. There was something weighty on his mind, and she just wished he would share his burden with her. If the patients could tell her their darkest secrets, and a great many of them did, then surely a psychiatrist could do likewise!

Wearily she flicked her hand through her hair, trying to push it back, forgetting for the moment that she'd had it cut. At least it was cooler, but she missed it. If she had hoped Jamie would comment on the new, more attractive style, she was to be disappointed. In a way, she had done it because of Paul. Now at last she was free of him and his constant demands, she wanted to become a new person—but a new person whom Jamie would come to love! And he never would.

It was lunchtime before she saw him again. This time he was in the company of Anne Redmond and one of the younger doctors at the General, who was doing a spell at the clinic—Peter Sayers, the same doctor she had seen Anne with at the barbecue. They were laughing and joking together, and Linda felt momentarily excluded. So when Miss Anstey sought her out and asked diffidently if she might share the table, she was delighted.

'There's no need to ask, Miss Anstey. All the patients share the staff canteen. You haven't got some infectious disease, and it's good to meet on a social basis, anyway.'

'Good therapy,' Miss Anstey said drily. She had been quieter even than usual lately, rather like Jamie. It must be the weather—it had been raining continuously for the past two days, and it had affected staff as well as patients.

'Never mind, once the weather brightens up again, we can go on another outing,' Linda consoled.

'I don't want to go on another outing, thank you, Sister, I intend to discharge myself,' Miss Anstey said firmly, stirring her tea vigorously. 'I don't believe the Clinic is doing anything for me—and I'm not ill, for goodness' sake!'

Taken aback, Linda sought for soothing words, but they didn't come immediately, and before she could comment, the woman had hurried out of the canteen, leaving her meal untouched. Linda went after her, but Jamie got there first. Between them, they managed to soothe her, but she was adamant that she wasn't attending any more. 'What good is it doing? If I'm not ill, then you can't cure me! Can you?' Her eyes begged Jamie for reassurance.

'In psychiatry, self-help is just as important as any help the professionals can give,' Jamie told her. 'Once you acknowledge that you *need* help, that's half the battle. If you keep on saying that you shouldn't be here and that you aren't ill and don't need help, then you won't improve—will you?' He waited while Miss Anstey considered this.

'I'm perfectly happy, really, Doctor,' she assured him. 'It's just sometimes, I——' She broke off, turning to Linda for reassurance.

'Just sometimes you need a helping hand, someone to talk to, perhaps a chance to cry?' Linda suggested, but Miss Anstey snorted.

'I never cry, it's a female weakness. No wonder men despise us!'

'Do they? *I* certainly don't despise women,' Jamie put in, with a chuckle. 'I rather like them!'

Miss Anstey smiled wanly. 'You're certainly a great favourite with your female patients, I'll grant you that!'

'And with the nurses too—we all adore Dr Grainger,' Linda told her, and saw Jamie's start of surprise. 'If you'd like to sit in the quiet room, I'll bring you some lunch on a tray and sit with you. I shan't be a minute.'

Leaving the patient with Jamie, Linda went back to the canteen, meeting Anne Redmond on her way out. The young doctor had disappeared, but the nurse gave her such a beaming smile that Linda wondered if there was some good news. 'You look happy,' she commented, as she arranged for another meal to be taken to Miss Anstey.

'Mm, so would you be. Well, I must get back—I'm afraid I'm going to be leaving, Sister. I know I've been here such a short time, but——' The nurse shrugged, then left the canteen, leaving a distraught Linda gazing after her.

It looked as though Anne was leaving to get married, and Linda supposed Peter Sayers was the lucky man, though it might be nothing of the sort, she told herself, scolding herself for over-using her imagination. But if it *was* the case, where would that leave Jamie? He had been fond of Anne, she was sure of it, and now. . .

Linda took Miss Anstey home after lunch, staying with her for a short time until the patient appeared more settled, and promising to return the following morning. She gained Miss Anstey's grudging permission to contact the community nurse, and she fully intended mustering all the services she could. She wished she could do as much for Jamie, reflecting as she drove back that Chrissie had let him down, no matter how much he had loved her, now Anne too—it was no wonder he had a somewhat jaundiced view of Linda herself! There must be some way of convincing him she genuinely loved him, wanted to care for him for the rest of their lives, but she couldn't see one right now.

He was holding a conversation with a child of about eight as Linda neared his office, and she paused. She had never seen him with a child before and presumed there wasn't room for them in his busy life. Pausing only to smile at them both, she hurried into her office, wondering who the little girl was.

She was on the telephone to one of her follow-up patients when Jamie appeared in the doorway, alone this time. He lounged there for a few moments, then frowned and walked away when Linda made no attempt to finish her conversation. That was typical of him! she fumed as she went in search of him a little later.

'I'm sorry, Doctor, but I was speaking to a patient—I could hardly cut him off in mid-sentence,' she pointed out. 'Who was the little girl? I didn't know you allowed children in,' she went on, remembering belatedly that she was meant to be soothing him, making him feel better about Anne's defection—she certainly wasn't making much of a job of it!

'A selection of expressions crossed your face then, Sister,' said Jamie, mildly enough. 'I thought at first you were going to choke me, but you changed your mind after a few seconds. Then,' he went on, getting up and gazing down at her, hands in pockets, 'you appeared to recall that I was a heartbroken man who needed plenty of tender loving care, and that whatever your grievances, you mustn't upset me. Am I right?' he challenged, and Linda squirmed, uncomfortable under his scrutiny.

'Partly, I suppose,' she amended. 'Anne Redmond said she was leaving and I thought——'

'You thought I was madly in love with her and must be a broken man because she's leaving to live with young Sayers when he goes back to London.'

'Is she?' Linda asked in surprise. 'I thought they must be getting married, she looked so happy.' She was unaware of the wistful note in her voice, but he picked it up immediately.

'Does getting married make people happy? I wonder,' he said reflectively, and Linda's heart ached for him.

'I think marriage is what most girls want, if they're really honest,' she parried. 'You told me once you loved your wife, so you must have been happy *some* of the time,' she went on, and he glanced at her sharply.

'Most of the time, actually, even though I knew she was the worst thing that ever happened to me. That's why I keep warning you about Paul Winterton—where is he, by the way?'

Jamie's gaze was intense, defying her to lie to him. 'To be honest, I don't know. He came back to collect the rest of his book, and I haven't seen or heard of him since,' she admitted.

'At least he hasn't gone back to Wanda's,' Jamie said grimly. 'I've been keeping a close eye on her and she's coming for a long weekend shortly—she wouldn't do that if Winterton was hanging around. That little girl, by the way,' he went on, 'is Muriel's grandchild. Her mother's in the General and there's no harm in the child coming here from time to time. I like children—do you?' It was an apparently casual question, but Linda saw the way his shoulders tensed, and knew her answer was important to him.

'Yes, very much—I enjoyed paediatrics when I was doing my general. Would you have liked children of your own?' she asked, knowing she was treading on dangerous ground.

'We nearly had one once—our son was stillborn. It was probably just as well, in the circumstances, but it affected Chrissie. Perhaps in some strange way a child would have touched a chord in her heart.'

A son—Jamie's son, Linda thought longingly. How perfect that would be! Instead she said, 'Wanda would have enjoyed being a grandmother. I'm sure children take to her instantly.'

Jamie nodded, but made no comment, just sat there staring into space, Linda herself apparently forgotten.

Feeling hurt, she moved towards the door, but his voice stopped her. 'Back to patient care, Sister—what do you think of Mrs Skilton's progress?'

'She's got on surprisingly well,' she admitted. 'She keeps telling me that Dr Grainger's a miracle-worker!' Gwen Skilton could be considered one of their successes. Once she had been put in a relaxed frame of mind, they had taken her through the list of situations she found difficult, beginning with the least alarming, like looking at pictures of people going in and out of shops, and eventually going on to situations where she actually had to leave her house, brave the cruel world beyond her front door. She still wasn't able to go out alone, but Linda felt they were well on their way. Once or twice she had even attended day patients, cat and all!

'We can't work miracles *every* day, but give her time and I think she'll come about,' Jamie commented. 'Miss Anstey is another problem to be solved, another patient we can't simply abandon, but on the whole we've had quite a good success rate—even before our new day patient sister arrived,' he added, a gleam in his eye.

Stung, Linda retorted, 'I never suggested you were a complete failure! But if the Clinic could expand, take in——'

'There you go again! Full of wild, impracticable schemes that we haven't the money for!' he said sharply.

Hands on hips, Linda glared at him, even though she privately conceded that he was right. 'But if we had a flag day, then there's the Garden Party——' she began, but he waved her down.

'Sit down, Sister, and let's discuss this calmly.' He pointed to the chair and Linda perched uneasily on its edge. 'Now, what's this about a garden party?'

'The Friends of the General Hospital—I belong to it,

and they have open gardens every now and again, to boost their funds. I thought if my neighbours opened *their* gardens, we could make a bit of money like that.'

A reluctant smile crossed Jamie's hard face. 'You're a busy little bee, Linda. I admire you for it, even though I doubt that even *half* your schemes would work. Never mind——' He held up a hand as Linda was about to speak again. 'Never mind, we'll try any idea you come up with. I owe you that, I suppose.'

'You don't owe me anything!' she flared. 'I——'

'There must be a lit fuse running between us, you know. It's never happened to me before. I keep wondering when it's going to blow us both sky-high,' he added, with a smile. 'I feel,' he went on slowly, staring into space, 'that all this emotion between us is ruining our professional relationship—and that can only be bad for the patients in the long run. Wouldn't you say?'

A feeling of cold dread settled on Linda's heart. He was asking her to leave! Not in so many words, perhaps, but that was obviously what he meant. 'But I enjoy our little arguments!' she wailed, then realised that it wasn't a professional remark to make. 'No, what I mean is, I thought an honest exchange of opinions was a good thing,' she amended quickly.

'Ah, so *that*'s what we have, is it?' Jamie's eyes were expressionless. 'And there I was, thinking they were heated arguments!'

'Well, they may have been occasionally,' Linda conceded, wondering how she was to extricate herself from the awkward position she'd got into. 'I'm sorry if I've spoken out of turn, but I believe in putting forward ideas if I think they're viable.'

'But some of your ideas just aren't viable, Sister,' he sighed. 'For instance, that idea you had about Nurse

Redmond and myself. Now *that* would never have worked. Since I haven't taken the slightest interest in her outside the Clinic, I can't imagine what put it into your pretty little head.'

'You took her out once! At least once,' she said hotly. 'You drove her away that evening she left early. Nurse Craig saw you,' she finished triumphantly. He couldn't fault Nurse Craig.

Jamie's face cleared, and he had difficulty in controlling his laughter. 'Nurse Redmond asked me for a lift, since we were going in the same direction. She was meeting Dr Sayers later, I believe. His salary doesn't run to a car,' he added drily.

'Oh! What about the "old friend" you visited at Stratford?' Linda hadn't meant to ask, the words just slipped out, and Jamie looked puzzled for a moment.

'Oh—*that* old friend! Auntie Hutton, I call her—she nursed my mother through her last illness.'

'Jumping to conclusions again,' Linda said slowly, feeling ashamed, then went to flick back a strand of hair. 'I keep thinking my hair's still long!'

'It looked lovely the way it was, Sister Scott. I don't recall your asking *my* permission to have it cut! Never mind, let it grow again,' he ordered, and her eyes flashed. Then she saw the glimmer of amusement in his own eyes, and nodded meekly.

'Yes, sir. I'll try to be more obedient in future, sir,' she murmured. Then her face clouded. 'That's if I *have* a future—were you suggesting that I leave the Clinic?' she asked bluntly. Better to know now that have him drop heavy hints until she finally *did* resign.

'There *are* other solutions,' he said mildly. 'If I didn't love you, it wouldn't matter too much. We could have a torrid affair and I'd get you out of my system, but as it is, Sister Scott——' He paused, and Linda's heart leapt at the expression in those sensuous eyes.

'I can quite see your problem, Dr Grainger, and if *I* didn't love *you*, I would be delighted with a torrid affair, too. But of course it wouldn't be professional,' she added, tongue in cheek, and Jamie laughed.

Then he held out his arms, and she went willingly into them, despite the fact that the office door was ajar and anyone could walk in. 'Sister Scott, I do believe I love you more each day,' he murmured against her hair.

'You have a strange way of showing it,' Linda couldn't help saying, as she raised her face for his kiss.

'Have I, my sweet? I'll have to do something about that, won't I? What would you suggest—give me the benefit of your advice again,' he went on, with a husky chuckle.

'That's it, keep mocking me! I like handing out advice,' she admitted. 'I must take after my old mum— she's always telling me how to run *my* life!'

'I admire your old mum, especially her cooking abilities! Do you suppose she'd like me to be her son-in-law?'

Jamie's eyes smiled into hers, and tenderly Linda stroked his dear, dear face. 'She keeps on about you. I think she rather fancied you,' she said pensively.

'I'm glad about that. I haven't any family of my own now, except for cousins, so I'll adopt yours—until we have one of our own,' he said gently, and Linda glanced away modestly.

'We'll have to see about that, Dr Grainger. I haven't decided yet,' she said firmly, then caught her breath as she was enveloped in a bear-hug.

'I think, despite that short fuse, we shall manage very well together,' he said with some satisfaction. Then, reluctantly, he released her. 'I've just remembered—Arundel Castle!'

'Richard the Third and the Duke of Norfolk,' Linda said dreamily. 'What about it?'

'I bought you a souvenir—a set of those pretty Wedgwood dishes. Seeing young Winterton when we got to Wanda's put it right out of my mind. Now, we ought to concentrate on the patients for the rest of the week. To work, Sister Scott!'

'Yes, Dr Grainger!' Linda laughed. Then there was a tap at the door, and Nurse Craig popped her head around it.

'I'm glad you're finished. I didn't like to interrupt you, but there's a telephone call for Sister on the outside line,' she added, beaming at them both. 'Should I offer congratulations?' she asked wistfully, and their answering smiles must have convinced her she should. 'You'll have a stormy marriage, but that's better than a placid one for folk like you,' she said comfortingly, then a smiling Linda followed her to the public telephone. Her happiness hadn't evaporated, but she had the dreadful feeling that it was going to. The only person likely to ring her at the Clinic was Paul.

'Are you sure you don't want me to go in with you?' Jamie asked as they neared the hospital, but Linda shook her head. This was one battle she had to fight by herself.

'No, I—I have to see Paul alone.' She managed a wan smile, then closed her eyes blissfully as Jamie's mouth met hers. 'Thank you,' she breathed, her eyes conveying her love. 'I'd better go in, see how he is, I suppose.' She was reluctant to leave the safety of Jamie's arms, but Paul needed her.

Torn two ways, she gazed back at Jamie as he waited

in the busy hospital corridor. 'I shan't be long.' She lifted a hand in farewell, then made her way to the ITU wondering what she would find.

That telephone call hadn't been from Paul himself, it was from Janice—Paul had been knocked down by a car and was in ITU near her home. After she had got over the shock, Linda had driven straight over to Shoreham to comfort his sister. Despite all their rows, she knew brother and sister were close. According to Janice, the injuries were severe and she was convinced her brother wasn't going to live. She was probably exaggerating in that way of hers, Linda thought, but Paul *could* be badly injured.

She was re-directed to Men's Orthopaedics, and that was where she found Paul, one leg in plaster, merrily regaling a sympathetic visitor with his story. He waved when he saw Linda, and she hurried over to him.

'Ah, this'll be your young lady, then,' the visitor said, getting up. 'I'm really here to see my husband, but this young lad's so brave, and so modest too! You must be proud of him,' the middle-aged lady beamed, before bustling away to a bed further down, and Linda looked at her in surprise.

'I was knocked down trying to save a dog,' Paul told her merrily.

'That I find hard to believe!' said Linda, sitting down in the chair the visitor had vacated. 'However, I'll take the story at face value! How are you, apart from the leg?'

'Pretty well, considering. I've been telling everyone the prettiest girl in the world is going to marry me, and they've all been clapping me on the back! Well, as far as they can,' he added brightly, and Linda's mouth tightened. Paul *was* in good form!

'I hope you find someone to marry you, then,' she said sweetly, 'because it certainly isn't going to be me!' On the way to the hospital, she had been turning over in her mind the best way to broach the subject of her forthcoming marriage to Jamie. If Paul had been seriously ill, then she wouldn't have told him. How could she have done? But now it was easier, and his face was a picture as she told him she was getting married.

'You've jilted me! How could you, Lindy!' His voice rose, but Linda waved him to silence.

'I haven't jilted you, I've never had the slightest interest in you as anything other than a friend, and if you go around telling people otherwise, I'll sue you for every penny that wretched book brings in!' she added sternly, and Paul looked crestfallen.

'No, I suppose you don't love me,' he admitted, then brightened as someone else approached the bed. 'This is Trudie, her brother's in here, but she really comes to see me!' he said smugly. 'Don't you, Trudie?' He held out his hand and the visitor took it.

Linda rose, smiling across at the girl who looked to be about twenty. 'Don't spoil him, Trudie, he'll take advantage of you!' she said lightly, then kissed her fingers before pressing them to Paul's brow. 'You'd better tell Janice how well you're feeling—she convinced me you were at death's door!'

With a wave, a happy Linda hurried to the door. Whatever Paul's problems were in the future, they were no longer hers, if ever they had been. She hoped Trudie wouldn't let him squeeze her dry as he had tried to do with herself and Wanda, but that lay in the lap of the gods.

Linda's particular problem rose as she pushed her way through the swing doors, and he was all she would ever need. Jamie's lopsided smile did strange things to her heartbeat, as she hurried into his arms, ready for a lifetime of storms together.

The door to her past awaited – dare she unlock its secrets?

AVAILABLE IN
FEBRUARY. PRICE £3.50

Adopted at sixteen, Julie Malone had no memory of her childhood. Now she discovers that her real identity is Suellen Deveraux – heiress to an enormous family fortune.

She stood to inherit millions, but there were too many unanswered questions – why couldn't she remember her life as Suellen? What had happened to make her flee her home?

As the pieces of the puzzle begin to fall into place, the accidents begin. Strange, eerie events, each more terrifying than the last. Someone is watching and waiting. Someone wants Suellen to disappear forever.

W◆RLDWIDE

**NEW
NEXT MONTH**

Follow the fortunes of love in our new zodiac romances.

Every month we will be featuring a new hero and heroine with different star signs as they embark upon the romance of a lifetime.

Discover whether they will find a match made in heaven or are destined to be star-crossed lovers!

Watch out for this new title amongst your Mills & Boon Romances from March.

4 MEDICAL ROMANCES
AND 2 FREE GIFTS
From Mills & Boon

Capture all the excitement, intrigue and emotion of the busy medical world by accepting four FREE Medical Romances, plus a FREE cuddly teddy and special mystery gift. Then if you choose, go on to enjoy 4 more exciting Medical Romances every month! Send the coupon below at once to:

**MILLS & BOON READER SERVICE, FREEPOST
PO BOX 236, CROYDON, SURREY CR9 9EL.**
No stamp required

✂ — — — — — — — — — — — — — — — — — ✂

YES! Please rush me my 4 Free Medical Romances and 2 Free Gifts! Please also reserve me a Reader Service Subscription. If I decide to subscribe, I can look forward to receiving 4 Medical Romances every month for just £5.80 delivered direct to my door. Post and packing is free, and there's a free Mills & Boon Newsletter. If I choose not to subscribe I shall write to you within 10 days – I can keep the books and gifts whatever I decide. I can cancel or suspend my subscription at any time. I am over 18.

Name (Mr/Mrs/Ms) ————————————————— EP02D

Address —————————————————————

——————————————————————————

————————————————— Postcode —————————

Signature ———————————————————————

— MEDICAL ♥ ROMANCE —

The books for your enjoyment this month are:

A DREAM WORTH SHARING Hazel Fisher
GIVE BACK THE YEARS Elisabeth Scott
UNCERTAIN FUTURE Angela Devine
REPEAT PRESCRIPTION Sonia Deane

♥   ♥   ♥   ♥   ♥

Treats in store!

Watch next month for the following absorbing stories:

CARIBBEAN TEMPTATION Jenny Ashe
A PRACTICAL MARRIAGE Lilian Darcy
AN UNEXPECTED AFFAIR Laura MacDonald
SURGEON'S DAUGHTER Drusilla Douglas